MERRY FRICKIN' CHRISTMAS

JODI JAMES

JAMES VENTURE PRESS

This book is dedicated to my grandfather who embodied the true spirit of the holidays. My childhood was filled with wonderful memories of him as Santa Claus. I was told stories of him in the Cedar Rapids Iowa holiday parade as Jolly Old St. Nicholas in the 1940's and 50's. He spent many years delivering gifts to a local orphanage and visiting families' homes for all the little boys and girls on Christmas Eve in his red suit and white beard. He looked forward to this every year, bringing him, and the masses so much joy.

INTRODUCTION

Award Winning Contemporary Romantic Suspense and Best-Selling author Jodi James expands her compelling heart-filled stories by adding Merry Frickin' Christmas in a fun, festive, Rom-Com.

Jodi writes about persevering through pain with positivity to find your passion. Her stories focus on tormented heroes who believe they're unworthy of love and the strong women who show them anything is possible.

ABOUT MERRY FRICKIN' CHRISTMAS

Christmas ignites in this opposites-attract, close-proximity entanglement, giving you all the feels. Sparks fly when Halo, holiday lovin' damsel in distress, finds herself in a head-on collision with Presley, a grumpy father of two. She rescues the day, rekindling the true meaning of the holiday spirit.

MERRY FRICKIN' CHRISTMAS

*A*s Presley DeVry rounded the corner onto his street, unending gunmetal grey clouds loomed overhead. Winters were so dismal, much like his mood.

He caught a glimpse of his neighbors, sisters Mavis and Mabel, hovering together, walking with slow, methodical movements until they saw him. Then the pep in their step changed.

"Nice timing," he said under his breath to no one.

The ladies were relentless in their constant matchmaking attempts. They had beaten him down more than once to go out on a date, both times disastrous. He wasn't ready to date, nor interested in just anyone.

He ducked, hoping by some miracle they wouldn't notice him. Fat chance of that with the size of his extended cab, Mazda Titan. The sisters were laser sharp. If he exited fast enough, maybe they wouldn't catch him?

Presley pulled into the driveway and tried to avoid eye contact as they scurried closer. He pulled out his phone and texted his cousin, who was watching the kids inside. Maybe she could intercept another onslaught.

Help! The sisters are at it again. You need to save me.

Poor baby. The big firefighter needs saving? she replied.

He covered his face and was blowing out a breath when a rap at the window startled him. He couldn't see anything but a bedazzled cane waving in the air.

"We see you. Are you trying to avoid us? Hello, you tall drink of water." Mavis' wavering voice was still plenty loud.

Presley winced and rolled down the window while his cousin Lauren snickered at the red front door of his white, single-story ranch. Presley could only see the tops of the ladies' heads, or their hair in this situation, which was teased sky high above them. He leaned out the window, recognizing their signature ruby red lips and thick, black-lined eyebrows. The only difference between the two women was Mavis had an inch or two height advantage. Their hair color, makeup, and clothes mirrored one another.

"You told us never to matchmake again, but we have the perfect woman for you. She's new in town and she delivers food to us. You just missed her," Mavis said.

He held up his hands. "Please, ladies, I don't think I can take anymore."

"Sugarboo, I'm telling you, this one is different! She's not like the others," Mabel pleaded. Her chin started wobbling.

Lauren must have taken pity on him at that point, because she lifted the garage door and yelled, "The kids need you inside! Hurry!"

"Excuse me." He rolled up the window, squeezing out the door when the sisters wouldn't budge. Opening the rear seat door, Presley grabbed his duffel bag, helmet, and gear. "Thanks, ladies. I'll get back to you. Gotta run."

"Please do. Such a handsome man shouldn't be alone."

"Alone? Kids and work keep me busy. I don't have time for anything else." *Lonely and alone are very different beasts. Lonely was the hollow chamber in his gut, the hunger that wouldn't go* away, a thirst that couldn't be quenched. In all the quiet, the loneliness was deafening.

"You need romance. We're too old for that, so we live vicariously through you."

"Ha! No thanks." He ran to his cousin, who had a cheesy grin on her face. "Thanks a lot. What took you so long? Are the kids okay?"

"They are just peachy. Loved seeing you sweat a little though."

He gave her a side squeeze and shook his head. "If I didn't love you so much, or owe you my life, I'd say a payback is in order."

"Whatever. You don't have a mean bone in you, but your 'tude might need a little tweak."

"My attitude is just fine."

"Hm... You're growlier than you used to be." She rolled her eyes and pivoted. "I'll grab my things. The kiddos are fed, teeth brushed, and ready for bed, but not asleep yet. They wanted to say goodnight to you."

* * *

PRESLEY TIPTOED THROUGH THE HOUSE, inching forward to the furthest end of the hallway and his son's bedroom, then peered into the doorway. Dillon was saying his nightly prayers at his Paw Patrol firetruck bed, the one he was outgrowing. "Big man in a little bed," he sang under his breath, and chuckled, thinking of an old late-night comedy skit.

"Please tell her I love her, and can you send her a message that we are okay and I'm being the big brother she asked me to be."

Presley stepped back with a gasp, rubbing at his chest. His heart still ached, especially for his children, and he suspected it always would.

He rapped on the door. "Time for bed, son."

The boy twisted around. His eyes were filled with tears.

Presley darted to his son and held him in his arms. "It's okay," he said as he soothed his son's back. "Shhh. I got you." He lifted his son and put him on his knee.

"I'm sorry, Daddy. I'm a big boy and I shouldn't cry." The boy wiped his face.

"Says who? I cry and I'm a really big guy."

"You do?" Dillon asked.

He nodded. "Absolutely."

"I never see you cry."

"I try not to in front of you. I get sad about Mommy even after three years." He had to be strong for them or he'd lose it.

His son squeezed him tighter. "You can always cry in front of me. I won't tell anyone. Pinky swears." He held out his little finger.

Presley looped his finger around his son's. "Thank you, Dillon. I'll remember that." He looked his son square in the eyes and lifted his chin. "You, too." Presley pulled the covers back and tucked his son in.

"Daddy. You're not going to die like Mommy did, are you?"

He struggled to swallow and cleared his throat. "Nope. Not for a long time."

"Do you think we will ever have a new mommy?"

"Oh, buddy. Your mommy will be yours forever. No one can ever replace her. Anyone who met you would love you like your mommy did. Maybe, when the right person comes along, they'll add to the love we already have."

"You're sad this time of year." Dillon watched him intently. "If a new mommy will make you happy, I want one for Christmas."

Dillon's simple statement hit Presley in the ticker like a pickax. He thought he'd hidden his emotions better. *Was I that obvious?* "How can I not be happy? I have the best kids ever."

After a few moments, Presley left Dillon's room, closing the door, and leaning against the wall. He rubbed his eyes, then peeked into Suzi's room. She was sound asleep under her LED-lit canopy, her cotton candy pink nightgown and her over-the-top bubblegum pink room screaming *I'm a princess and don't you ever forget it*. Her dark blonde Fraggle-Rock hair was out of its normal pigtails. As he tiptoed forward, he eyed something clutched against her chest in her tiny little hands.

It was the last family photo they had taken when Abby had been pregnant with Suzi. He wiggled the frame from her grasp and set it on her nightside table, replacing it with her Pepto-colored unicorn. Suzi had been so young when Abby died, most of her memories were of her mother being sick.

He walked into his bedroom, turning on the big screen television and the overhead ceiling fan. It was the noise he needed to get through the long nights. He heard scratching, followed by a whimper at the door, and he let Champ in. The hundred-pound golden retriever showed no sign of ever getting through the puppy stage, with a perma-smile on his face and a penchant for getting into everything. Big dark eyes assessed him. Sometimes he thought the dog would start talking. *Maybe I'm losing it. Or maybe I'm just that lonely.*

Kicking off his boots, Presley eased back on the bed, grabbing the remote and channel surfed for something mindless. Christmas was days away. How would he ever pull this off and make it special for the kids?

Champ bounced all over the bed, trying to retrieve his latest favorite chewy toy, one that hadn't already been spliced, diced, and gutted. The dog was relentless. This could go on for hours.

"Good boy," he said, ruffling Champ's fur. Some of the tension slipped out of him. How could he not smile when this dog was so happy?

Leaping off the bed, Champ burrowed into the far corner of the closet and came up with one of Abby's shoes, one Presley had missed. He knew he needed to donate the last of her clothes. After all, they had been bagged up for the past year and a half. But there was a finality to the action, and he couldn't bring himself to do it.

Maybe that's why his dates never worked out. He didn't want them to. One day, he'd get the balls to move on. Shifts at the firehouse were a hell of a lot less complicated than dating. At least at work, his mind was on his career and saving lives.

HALO WRIGHTWAY PULLED the last of the boxes and garbage bags from her car and into her tiny new studio apartment. She hadn't had time before taking a last-minute seasonal job delivering meals to the elderly in Spirit Pines, Iowa, her new home for the foreseeable future. There was a sense of freedom that came with the endless rolling hills and open country. The world was hers! She would even be starting her dream job after the holiday break.

Singing *I Will Survive* at the top of her lungs, Halo danced along to the oldie but goodie, then spun around, throwing a crumpled newspaper into the trashcan.

"Score!"

She pumped a fist in victory. A new beginning was just what she needed. Being uprooted and alone was in her DNA.

"Alone isn't so bad. I've been there, done that." She straightened her posture and lifted her chin. "I got this," she said to herself as she shimmied across the room to change the music. The new song inspired more singing. "I'm dreaming of a White Christmas, just like the ones I've never known. Squee…"

UGH. Presley shook his head. His captain had insisted that his upcoming sabbatical was years overdue, something about sensitivity guidelines and an attitude overhaul. But getting the kids ready on this last day before it started was like herding goats. Thankfully, Lauren's place, their home away from home during his long shifts at the fire station, wasn't far.

Dillon was balancing his spoon on his nose when he wasn't slurping his cereal, only to drop it over and over with a clank and milk spillage. Suzi wore a peanut butter mask, including a stray banana slice under one eye, while she played Cheerio toss with Champ.

Presley felt like he should be annoyed, but he laughed. They were his saving grace. He eyed his watch. "Let's go, troops. Daddy's going to be late."

"Are you riding in the fire truck?"

"Rrrr—Rrrr—Wooo..." Suzi chimed in with a giggle.

"Not today. I just need to do a few things and then I'll be home for the holiday."

"Yay!" the kids cheered, spreading more food into the glorious mess.

Presley took a deep breath and redirected their focus to something less messy. "You know, Santa's coming. We need to decorate the tree."

"Daddy, that tree is yucky," Suzi said, swiping at the banana on her face.

"Maybe the decorations will help?"

"Santa Claus is coming to town," Dillon sang. Suzi clapped and stood on her chair.

"Oh, no you don't, little one. Be careful." Presley tugged at the towel he had on his shoulder, wiping his little girl's hands and face before wrapping her in her pink coat. He swiped his palm over her corn silk hair and tied on her matching pink stocking cap.

"Nice pipes, Dillon." He gave his son a high-five. "The sooner we leave, the quicker I can get home. There's a snowstorm coming tonight."

Champ jumped up on the table and licked up the Cheerios that hadn't already made it to the floor or their mouths.

"Snow? Yippee, a white Christmas. Snow angels!" Suzi cheered.

"I'll help you." Dillon grabbed their backpacks. "Us big boys have to stick together."

"We sure do." He tapped his son's freckled nose.

* * *

THE CHILL SHOT straight through Halo's bones, whipping right around the walls of the warehouse. Pausing to run her hands over her arms for warmth, Halo took a second, then continued to stack boxes and bags into her car for her elderly patrons. The skies were dark, and the clouds looked angry. Huge flakes floated down like white confetti.

Halo danced around to the other side of her car, tugging at her clothes. Maybe she had been overzealous when she'd layered up. She knew she looked like one of those blow-up yard decorations. She fastened the seat belt, then inch-wormed three miles to the only neighborhood she had ever traveled to in her new town.

Sliding around the corner as her tires plowed through the snow made Halo bite hard and grind her back molars.

"Snowpocalypse!"

Her back end fishtailed to the left, then shimmied to the right. Clutching the steering wheel, Halo's heart thumped wildly and battered her breastbone as her car did a slow donut.

"HALP!" she shrieked, followed by a nervous laugh.

The tires spun as she hit the gas, throwing chunks of snow in her wake. There was no way she'd make it up the hill to the last two houses on her route. Nevertheless, she'd climb Mount

Everest to get her elderly shut-ins the Christmas holiday meals they deserved.

Wiping the condensation off the windows, she squinted through the windshield and decided her car had gone far enough.

"Good times."

Stumbling out, Halo nearly face-planted into a nearby pile of snow. She loaded up the last two bags and slogged through the ankle-deep white stuff that now covered the landscape. Snowflakes landed on her lashes and the visibility was sketchy, but she closed her eyes and took it all in. There were going to be many firsts. Her breath lingered in puffs as she clutched the bags closer.

WHY HAD he waited so long to prepare? No matter how much Presley dreaded this time of year, it wasn't the children's fault. Besides, Abby had loved the holidays. She'd haunt him like Jacob Marley if he didn't whip it in shape.

Presley traipsed through the Super Mart, where wide-eyed customers bobbed and weaved around in a frenzy. Checkout lines snaked around the store with overfilled shopping carts. He wanted to puke the minute he heard the Christmas music.

How could one person do such an about-face? This was not him.

He dug at his chest, wiping off the beads of sweat littering his forehead, and grabbed a small basket, only to return and get a cart when it got too heavy to carry. Whipping around the store in record time, Presley power shopped for every toy, doll, and gadget he'd seen on recent commercials, plus a heaping pile of a little of this and a lot more of that.

On the way home, Presley turned up the radio for the national weather report. *Twelve to sixteen inches projected overnight.* He bet the boys at the station would love their shift.

At the bottom of the hill was a beat-up car he didn't recognize. What were people thinking? That vehicle wasn't worthy of Midwest winters.

* * *

HALO INHALED, then coughed when the arctic air smacked her in the lungs. Hauling the meals up the hill in almost a foot of snow was a full-body workout.

Note to self, get in shape!

The sky dam had busted open. Snow was blowing sideways, swirling, and dancing around. *Freak-out time.* Her pulse rapped a staccato as she dashed over to the sisters' house, slipping every few steps. During her last visit, Halo had ducked and avoided their assault as they fired personal questions at her, so many that she suspected an investigation was underway. The ladies had tried to set her up, and the last thing she needed was a complication. Not after her ex. No. Thank. You.

Thick, wet snow caked her boots as she skated her way to their front door. If she ever got out of here, she'd have to remind someone about shoveling their snow. Halo rang the bell and Mavis answered the door.

"Come on in, honey bunny. You'll catch frostbite."

"If I stay here any longer, I'll be spending the holidays with you." Before she knew it, Halo was yanked into the house by both women.

"Nonsense. You need to warm yourself up and have some tea."

"I need to drop this off and get home if my car will cooperate. I have your meals for you, plus a little gift."

"We didn't get you anything." One said with a heavy sigh as the other lay a hand over her breastbone.

"Holidays are for giving! I expect nothing in return. Christmas is about love." Halo set the large bag of food down and dug for a tin of shortbread cookies. "Here. It's not much." She handed it to one woman.

"But it is more than you think it is to us, right, Mavis?" Mabel asked. Mavis nodded.

"I understand from personal experience about small acts of kindness a time or two in my life. I want to pay it forward." Halo thought of her great-aunt and held back the tears threatening to spill from her eyes. "Please let me carry this heavy bag in for you. There are three meals and all the heating instructions you need for the holidays." She hoisted the bag onto the kitchen table.

"Are you sure you can't stay for some tea and your cookies?"

"I'm so inexperienced driving in the snow, I have knee-knocking palpitations at the moment." She treaded to the front door. The exterior door was covered with something like another layer of glass. "What is that?" She gulped down a breath and pointed with a shaky digit.

"Oh, dear," Mabel said as her eyes narrowed. "Freezing rain. You don't want to drive on a sheet of ice like this."

"Ice? I must get home before this gets worse."

Waving at the sisters, Halo clomped out the door, took a few steps, lost her footing, and slid down the driveway.

"Whoa! Wheee…" she screamed, partly from shock and partly from the exhilarating ride. She shot up only to fall again, this time into a snowdrift. "That's going to leave a mark."

Halo patted the slush off her backside, but it stuck to her in globs. Sleet spit at her face like tiny needles, nearly blinding her. The streetlight reflected against the fresh snow like thousands of glimmering crystals, looking far too friendly compared to what she was experiencing. She ambled her way to her car, sending positive energy into the universe. After all, it was two days before Christmas, nearly dark, and her clunker was as unpredictable as this weather.

"Here's hoping we can get this show back on the road. Fingers crossed."

* * *

PRESLEY SET his kids at their little crayon-colored table with lidded cups of hot cocoa. "I'll make you a PB& J. Be good and don't get into trouble. Just watch the movie." He queued up *Phineas and Ferb.* "I need to unload the rest of the stuff out of the truck. Maybe we can decorate the Christmas tree later," he called over his shoulder.

Crickets…

Presley stepped back into the room.

"Dillon, you're in charge. Come get me if you need anything. I won't be very long." The kids were transfixed. When he stopped the movie, all eyes locked on him. "Dillon, Suzi, did you hear me?" They both gave him a blank stare and looked at each other. "Eyes forward." He pointed to his peepers and back to theirs.

"Daddy, I'll babysit Suzi and watch the movie with her."

"I'm not a baby."

"Thank you, Dillon. Suzi, be a good little princess and listen to your brother."

Presley slipped on his heavy parka and stocking cap. Punching the garage open, he noticed someone in his peripheral vision tromping through the snow. Maybe it was the owner of the stranded vehicle just beyond his driveway.

Presley waited to see if the car would start. After almost flooding the engine, it finally did. He grabbed a few shopping bags out of his truck and took them into the house.

When he came back out a few minutes later, the vehicle was still idling. At this point, the car had about a foot of snow on it and the windows were covered with ice. Having lived here most of his life, he knew they'd probably stay that way. He went back into the garage, grabbed a push-broom and his mack-daddy ice scraper, before wandering across the street.

"Hey, do you need any help?"

"Holy shite! You scared me half to death," the bundled-up person screamed, sounding like she was just barely holding it together. She whipped around.

It was difficult to see anything under the crocheted hat, the giant scarf, and the enormous amount of winter wear in every color of the rainbow, but Presley knew he would never forget the color of her vivid, shamrock-hued eyes. They were captivating.

He shook off his scrambled thoughts. "It's—it's a little cold out here. Um—thought you could use a hand." His tongue tripped all over his teeth. *Smooth.*

"A little cold? It's frigid enough to freeze the balls off a pool table."

"What?"

"Never mind. I'm waiting for the windshield to clear, but it's taking longer than a three-toed sloth."

Presley chuckled. "In this weather, not likely to happen at all. As soon as it melts, it freezes again. Do you have a scraper?"

"No. I wasn't exactly prepared for the snow," she said as she jumped from foot to foot and flailed her arms.

"Let me help." He raised the scraper he was holding. "Good thing I'm prepared. I live over there." He pointed to his house. "You take the broom and push some of the heavy snow off your car and I'll scrape the ice if I can."

* * *

"Thank you."

Yabba-dabba-dude, he was handsome. A dark shadow of stubble roughened his strong jawline and prominent cheekbones. His dirty blonde hair had enough length to peek out from his stocking cap. Fierce eyebrows slashed across his fore-head. His dark, sullen eyes were as turbulent as a storm, but held a familiar mixture of anguish and torment. An attempt to smile, mixed with undeniably sexy despair, felt contradictory, but at least he was trying. Halo's heart warmed with understanding.

"What are you doing out on a day like this?"

"Last minute deliveries."

"Haven't seen you around. New here?" His tone was forward and direct.

"I just moved here last month. I wanted seasonal work until my other job starts after the first of the year."

"Where?" he yelled over the wind in his smoky voice. Long dormant feelings woke up to the soothing sound.

She moved closer. "I'll be the new kindergarten teacher at the elementary."

"You're taking over for Miss Penelope at Cedar Ridge?" Her new hero rubbed his hands together. "My son is in her class."

Double poo! Of course. He has a family, and I'm sure his wife is a supermodel. What was I thinking?

He leaned in, using his muscular arms and brawny shoulders to penetrate the ice-coated windshield. "I don't think you're going anywhere. As soon as I clear your windshield, it freezes up again. Turn your defrost on full blast and let's get out of the cold."

She stared at him, hoping her arching brow and lack of a poker face weren't noticeable. "I couldn't." More like she wouldn't. What if he was a mass murderer or something?

His eyes met hers with a cursory glance. "You'll freeze to death. My conscience can't leave you out here and my kids are probably dismantling the house right now. Warm up and we can try this again in a few minutes."

Halo followed her rescuer to his house in short, duck-like steps. The driveway was steep, and she couldn't gain traction.

Suddenly, she was doing a cartoon-worthy slip, slide, and away with her feet. "Whoa!"

He stretched out his gloved hand. The sensation of his powerful grasp sent a seismic jolt through her entire system.

Safe. She was safe.

What the hell? He's a married man with children. Reality check, girlfriend.

Halo slid backward like a conveyor belt in reverse. She was feet over face in a split-second, hitting her head on the snow-packed concrete. This was not her idea of knocking some sense into herself.

"Are you okay?" he asked as he knelt over her.

Did I black out?

She squinted, then blinked to gain focus. His face was so close to hers, she could feel his warmth, and as the blur burned off, she could see his oceanic blues. "Is this heaven?"

"Nope. Last I checked, it's Iowa." His brows furrowed and worry etched his face. "You smacked your head hard."

"Iowa?" She crinkled her face, closed her eyes, then opened them again as she rubbed the painful part on the back of her head. "Ouch. When I do things, I do them epically full-blown."

"I'll help you up." He pulled her to her feet. The earth moved, and she wobbled to stay upright.

"There's two of you." She closed one of her eyes. "Must leave." She clung to him tight, and though said the words, she didn't budge.

"You could have a concussion. I have a medical background. No arguments. Inside. Now."

The caveman thing kindled a spark in her belly.

* * *

Presley tucked the woman close. Her body trembled, her teeth chattered, and she swayed. Sensations flooded him. He was hyper-aware of his task and his oath to help those in need.

He entered through the kitchen, still holding her hand, and pulled her hat off. Blonde hair flowed from underneath, brighter at the ends, and sweeping across her forehead just over her heart-shaped face. "Good, you're not bleeding."

He unzipped her coat, only to find several more layers, each one as vibrant as the next. "Good thing you had all this extra padding."

"I look like an Oompa Loompa." She made a goofy face.

He fumbled with the buttons and zippers. "It may have saved you from further injury." When she unraveled the scarf, he saw the smooth column of her neck. Her dainty fingers shook as she untangled a long silver locket of jade, the pendant the same color as her eyes. Her light skin was free of makeup, but her glowing cheeks were crimson from the cold. She was more delicate than he'd expected, willowy even. Her expression beamed.

He stood, mesmerized, greedily drinking in the view.

The moment broke as the dog barked and the kids squealed. Presley pulled out a chair. "Be right back." He leaned around the corner. "What's going on? I thought you were watching a movie." Catching sight of the dog, Presley had to chuckle. "You're kidding me. Champ, I'm sorry buddy, you poor thing."

Champ now sported Presley's baseball jersey, a pink tutu, and Dillon's spaceman helmet from Halloween. The dog whined and panted. "Poor boy."

"Daddy, I got my helmet stuck on Champ's head!" Dillon yelled as Suzi added a strand of colorful beads and a pink fur boa around the dog's neck.

Presley turned back to the woman and pointed in the kids' direction. She glanced around the corner wide-eyed and snorted, followed by her hee-haw laugh.

"Welcome to my world." He rolled his eyes. "I'll get you

something for your head as soon as I save my emasculated dog." Sighing, he tromped into the other room, calling, "Suzi Abigail, leave that poor dog alone."

HALO RUBBED her temples and took a deep breath, but she couldn't resist another look. The man was bent over, yanking the helmet off the dog's head. He'd lost his footing, retreated from helmet removal, and turned to wrestling the clothes off the enormous pet. A little girl, who looked to be around four and had pink lipstick smeared over half her face, had her arms around the animal, giving him kisses. The boy jumped on his dad's back, riding him like a stallion.

Halo's heart warmed. This was home, chaos and all, the center of all her fantasies of life when you had a family. A life she wished for but had never manifested.

She sneezed, and suddenly all attention was on her. The boy, probably six, dismounted from his dad's back just as the dog lunged forward, wagging his tail at warp speed. She backed away and lost her footing on the wet floor. Champ toppled over her, pinning her down, and rewarded her with an ample face saturation with his mammoth tongue.

"Some guard dog you are. Champ, get off our guest."

"It's okay. I love dogs. This is a dog, right?" Halo said, giggling and wiping off her cheeks.

The boy tried to wrestle the dog off by his collar, to no avail. The father let out a piercing whistle and guided the dog away.

Halo examined the little girl, who now had her arms wrapped around her dad's long legs. Despite missing two front teeth, the girl's smile lit up the room, her cherub cheeks rosy. Her delicate blonde hair floated around a crooked princess crown. The little boy sported an impressive chocolate milk mustache and a superhero cape.

"Who's that, Daddy?" the little girl asked, pointing.

"This is..." He scratched his head. "I didn't get your name." The father reached for her hand.

She righted herself and smoothed her clothes. "My name is Halo."

"Like on an angel?" the little girl said.

"Yes, I guess. Halo Wrightway. And you're...?" she asked, turning to the dad.

He reached for a glass of water sitting on the table, took a gulp before replying. "Presley DeVry."

Halo snickered. "Like blue suede shoes?"

"Yes, like the king of rock-and-roll. My mom had an obsession." He took another drink.

"I love it. *Thank you, thank you very much.*" She did her best Elvis impersonation, lip curl and all.

Presley spit out his water and coughed. "You're killing me. Good one."

"Daddy." The boy shimmied his way in between them. "My name is Dillon. I'm the big brother."

"Yes, you are, and the best one ever." His father ran his fingers through his son's dark hair, which was full of cowlicks.

"This is my sister, Suzi. Pink is her favorite color."

"Kids, let's give Miss Wrightway time to breathe. She fell outside and I need to get her an ice pack for her head."

"A boo-boo, Daddy?" the little girl asked.

"I really should go. I don't want to intrude on your family." She wrung and twisted her hands together, glancing at her watch.

"Nonsense. After our best try at being a stellar welcoming committee, you'd want to leave?"

She chuckled, "Best welcome by far."

Halo couldn't help watching his every move, even when he was just digging around in the freezer.

"We saved our best stuff for you." He handed her a bag of

frozen peas. "This will feel better on your head than an ice pack."

Halo touched the back of her head and winced. "Thank you."

"I'll grab some aspirin, too." He eyed her straight on. "Look at me."

She did, but his direct gaze made her blush, so she turned away, yanking at her collar.

Presley guided her chin forward again. "Remember how I mentioned I have medical training? I'm experienced in this kind of stuff."

"He's a firefighter! He can save your life if you need him to," Dillon said.

"A firefighter, huh? I'm fine."

"We have to rule out serious symptoms. You don't appear to have any slurred speech. Nausea? I don't think you lost consciousness. Do you still see double?"

She shook her head from side to side, warmed just by his proximity. Thank God she wasn't seeing double, or she'd be toast. "Just a minor bump and pride shamefully bruised."

Presley pulled out two chairs and lifted both kids to their seats. They gawked intently at Halo, but Presley stepped to the window and glanced at the clouds. "I don't suspect you're going anywhere, between the weather and your head injury."

"I should go before your wife comes home."

* * *

Presley jolted and eyed the children. *What did she say?* He scrunched his eyelids closed and bowed his head. He always dreaded the look in everyone's eyes when they heard he lost his wife.

Pity. He hated their pity. Over the years it was easier focusing the attention onto the children than on himself.

"Mommy doesn't live here anymore. She's in heaven," Dillon said, lowering his head. His lower lip stuck out.

"She watches over us," Suzi added.

* * *

HALO GASPED. She couldn't speak, let alone swallow the golf-ball-sized lump in her throat. Her heart ached.

Open mouth, insert foot. What a pudding head.

She turned to Presley, who was holding the bridge of his nose. "I'm so sorry. I'm always saying something without thinking. It's a gift."

"It's okay." He attempted a smile. "You had no way of knowing."

She wanted to sob for the kids. They were so young. And for him, losing his wife so early. A tear slipped from the corner of her eye, but she swiped it away.

"You are so lucky to have a guardian angel. You must be really special." Halo poked the little girl in the stomach, and she giggled.

Presley cleared his throat and paced the room. "I better turn off your car and lock it."

"No." She stood and got dizzy, but used the table to steady herself.

"You are not driving. I'll only be a moment."

"I'm tougher than I look." No truer words were spoken. She had to be. "Don't worry, the kids will be fine."

"It's not them I'm worried about." He chuckled. "Back in a flash."

"I want fishy food," Suzi announced. She sprang off her chair and darted to the kitchen pantry, then to the refrigerator. Arms full of crackers and juice, the little princess surged forward. Before Halo could register a thing, Suzi tripped and then everything seemed to happen in slow motion. Little orange guppies flew all over the floor. The juice sprayed all over the three of them as they stood there, stunned. Champ went into dog chomp mania to get to the crackers.

"I did an oopsie," Suzi whimpered, putting a hand to her hair.

"It's okay, whoopsies happen." Halo grabbed a nearby dishcloth and tried to get the sticky off.

Dillon sprinted over to his little sister and helped her up. She was rubbing her knee, and the boy kissed it. Suzi moaned and rubbed her dirty hands.

Presley opened the door and froze when he saw goldfish crackers swimming in a red sea.

Halo winced and pushed her wet hair away. "She helped herself to snacks, but they didn't make it to their destination." Halo grimaced and raised her shoulders to her earlobes. "Your daughter is going to need a bath. There's goo everywhere." Taking a breath, she shooed him off with authority. "Go on. I'll clean up Dillon and this mess."

"Bossy, aren't we?" He picked up his daughter and saluted Halo. "Come on, Little, we have marching orders. Time for a rub-a-dub-dub."

* * *

"DADDY, IS SHE YOUR GIRLFRIEND?" Suzi asked as she pushed her mermaid along the water.

"No, sweetie. I just met her. Her car broke down, remember?"

"It's okay if she is. I know Mommy wouldn't mind. She's nice."

"I'll always love your mom. Yes, Miss Wrightway is very nice."

"She is pretty, too, don't you think so?"

"Yes, but no one can steal my heart but you." He piled

shampoo on his daughter's hair and lathered it around, making it stand up on the ends. "You are my sunshine, my only sunshine, you make me happy..." he whispered.

The floorboard creaked, and he swung around.

"I didn't mean to interrupt."

He got up and opened the door further. "Miss Wrightway."

"Please call me Halo. We are far beyond formalities. What's it been, years?" she said as she blew her bangs away.

"Ages. Some first meet, huh? Give me a minute." Presley went back and poured a pitcher of water over his daughter's hair, then leaned over her to drain the water out of the bathtub. "Bath time is over, pumpkin. We have lots to do tonight." He wrapped her in a towel. "Snug as a slug bug in a rug."

"You funny, Daddy. It's a towel! And I'm not a bug." Suzi giggled.

* * *

HALO PULLED at her shirt and got a good whiff and gagged.

"Hey."

She backed away. "Don't get too close. I smell. I need to go."

"About that. Your battery is dead. I called for roadside service while I was outside, and the dispatcher said no one was getting anywhere tonight. The weather service announced severe conditions and banned all travel because of below zero windchill and icy roads. I called the station, and there are cars stranded everywhere. They're predicting more sleet, snow, and a severe weather bomb cyclone."

"Wait. A what? A bomb? How did you get all that information with one phone call?"

"I have connections." He pointed to his helmet and duffle bag with the Maltese Cross emblem. "This bomb cyclone is new to me too, but my buddies in Colorado got hit with one and it packed a punch. Have you seen it outside recently?"

"But... I can't stay here."

"Why not?"

"It's almost Christmas, and..."

Presley spread his open hands, gesturing to the room. "Don't leave me alone. The kids have an advantage. I'm begging you." He put together his hands like he was praying, then raised a brow and grinned.

She laughed. "You have a point."

"It's safe, warm, and I have a spare room in the basement with a bathroom and a lock on the door. I even swore an oath to help the citizens of our city." He placed a hand over his heart.

"You rescued this unprepared citizen from peril before Christmas," Halo said with a laugh.

"I have a feeling you might be doing the rescuing." Presley winked. "Tis the season to be jolly, and all the peace on earth, mumbo jumbo."

"You are not an Ebenezer, are you?"

"Sorry. I have my bah humbug moments." He crossed his arms over his chest, and Halo noticed how it made his muscles flex.

"I'm a big holiday fanatic. I will pay my debt for your hospitality and help you get in the spirit. Do we have a deal?" She stretched out her hand. "Let's shake first."

"Absolutely." They lingered there for a moment.

Halo reluctantly slid her hand away. "I—I need to get something out of my car. I brought a few clothes, so I can change."

"Not tonight."

"Why?"

"It would take a torch, plus the cutters and spreaders, to open your doors. Frozen shut as soon as I turn the engine off and locked it. You may end up in the next county with the wind blowing like it is, anyway."

"I'm gross. My clothes are stuck to me."

Presley looked around and snapped his fingers. "I have a few things I'm donating. They were my wife's. You can have whatever you want."

"No. I couldn't." She grimaced. *No.* Just the thought felt every which way of wrong. *Yikes.*

"It's okay. Really. I admit it's been a slow process, and every time I think I'm done, I find something else tucked away. Seriously, she was a clothes hoarder. Getting down to this last load has a sense of finality to it, and I can't think of a better use for them."

Halo covered her face and dropped her head. She felt his pain. "I'd be okay with just an old t-shirt."

"Nonsense. You can have it all. You'd be doing me a huge favor. If my wife was still here, she'd give you the clothes off her back anyway. Please."

He looked at her with such warmth and adoration, talking about his late wife. How could she say no? Halo nodded.

"I'll leave a few towels in the spare bathroom, so you can clean up and bring the clothes down. Take your time. We're not going anywhere."

* * *

PRESLEY'S BREATH hitched when she walked into the kitchen. Halo's hair was in two braids and a backward ball cap. She had a yellow t-shirt that said *bed hair don't care*, and baggy tangerine-colored sweats rolled up at the bottom. She bit at her thumbnail and tugged at the clothes, but they suited her. Halo looked like a ray of sunshine, showing off the natural beauty that had intrigued him at first glance. Sparkling eyes, creamy skin, a sense of humor, and true grit.

"What can I do?" she asked, rubbing her hands together.

"You can get the paper plates and plastic silverware for the kids."

She put them on the counter. "Okay, now what?"

"Relax." He tried to guide her to a seat.

"*Moi?*" She eyed the pudding box on the counter. "Nope, I'll take on dessert."

"You got it." He grabbed a bowl, whisk, and a gallon of milk, setting it all in front of her. They moved around the kitchen with ease, as if they've done it for years. "Why were you out driving in this weather?"

"I was delivering meals to your neighbors for the holidays."

"Nice. You took over the route? What do you think of Mabel and Mavis?"

"Those women are friendly, but come on a little too strong. The last time I delivered, they almost dragged me out to meet someone. I barely got away with my arm intact."

Presley covered his mouth with his hand and blew out a breath, then chuckled. "I think they mentioned you."

"No way. You?" She propped her hand on her hip.

"More than likely. I'm their most recent charity case."

"Interesting." A flush crept across her cheeks, and she tucked her hair behind her ear.

"Mavis and Mabel love romance. Everyone calls them the Matchmaking Divas, and they take the title very seriously. You've been warned."

"Good to know."

"Where are you from?" Presley asked as he turned back to loading chicken nuggets on a baking sheet.

"Somewhere where it doesn't snow. I'm originally from Mississippi, but for the last eight years I lived in south Florida." The soft sound of the whisk against the bowl reached Presley's ears.

"Weather shocker, right?"

"A wee bit." She held up her hand, measuring an inch with her thumb and forefinger, and winked.

"You get used to it, but the town shuts down when it gets this bad. That's why I wouldn't be in any big hurry. They'll get to your car when they get to it. Throw the holidays on top of it and you might be stranded here until after the first of the year."

Her mouth hung open, whisk hanging forgotten above the bowl. "You're flipping kidding me!"

"Wish I was."

"I can't possibly stay here that long."

"Sure, you can." He had to admit he enjoyed having her around, but he knew he had to explain a little more. "I lost my wife around Christmas." He backed against the wall, needing something solid to hold him up.

Halo dropped the whisk and hugged herself. "How long since she passed?"

"Three years, but she was sick before that." He unconsciously moved toward her. She was easy to talk to. "I want to make the holidays right for the kids. They don't deserve my hang-ups. I thought I was doing a good job hiding it until recently. Dillon is very observant." He had a sour taste in his mouth and an ache in the back of his throat. "I need them to have happy memories of Christmas, like I did as a child. I'm not proud of myself."

"You can never bury your feelings. They crap slap you." She nodded and swung her fists together. "True story."

"You say the funniest things, but they make total sense."

"Good! Someone finally understands my humor." She looked him right in the eyes. "Together we will make this Christmas one they will remember for a lifetime."

She made him want to believe in miracles. Presley paused and gazed into her jewel-toned green eyes, fringed with lush lashes. It had been so long since anyone interested him. He wanted to kiss her dainty little nose, but felt the color leave his face. He wrapped his hand around hers and... had no clue where his next thought was. His brain was blank.

Presley's blood soared through his veins; his heart pounded so loudly in his ears that he thought he might go deaf. There was an unfamiliar lightness in his chest. He yearned for more. For her.

He released her hand but wanted to immediately grab it again. All his senses were heightened. He jerked back and cleared his throat. Inhaled deep and swallowed hard.

* * *

PEACE COCOONED HER. "PRESLEY." Halo rasped. His eyes gleamed a dazzling blue, unlike before, as an internal switch flipped. She bit her bottom lip. The way he looked at her was like he was reaching into the depths of her soul.

"What? Uh—sorry." His chin dipped and his posture slumped. He hurried to the sink and latched his grip on the countertop. She watched him carefully, wringing her hands. The look on his face pulled on her heartstrings.

Ensnared by what she saw in his expression, she realized no one had ever looked at her that way. Her ex had barely looked at her–he was more into his video games and nights out with the guys, just using her for what little money she made. That first time he had manhandled her was the last. There had been no soul-connecting gazes.

Presley wiped moisture from his lip with his sleeve. "I'll drag the tree inside later and get the decorations. I promised the kids they could decorate it tonight."

Suddenly, the oven timer went off, making them jump.

"Can you pull the dinosaur nuggets out of the oven while I finish the cheesy mac?" Presley handed her an oven mitt and smiled, showing his killer pearly whites. Adrenaline rushed through her, and she had to wave the potholder across her face.

"Hope you're hungry. I pulled out all the stops."

She laughed, then put the completed pudding in the refrigerator. "I've eaten a few oddly shaped nuggets in my day." She blew on it, then popped one in her mouth. "I'll cook tomorrow."

He didn't hesitate. "Twist my arm."

She grabbed his arm, the contact stirring tingles across her nerves.

Presley relented with a grin. "Okay, okay. If you insist." He grabbed his arm in jest.

Her breath quickened, and she shivered. Her lips parted, but she couldn't articulate a single syllable.

* * *

Presley returned with lights and ornaments, quickly setting the tree into the stand. After securing the tree, he scooted out from under and bumped into Halo.

"Hey there," he said breathlessly, then recovered himself and called, "Kids! Let's decorate the tree."

Suzi dove into the box, pulling out a strand of silver garland and wrapped it around her shoulders. "See me?"

"You look pretty, baby girl, but let's put it on the tree."

"I'm helping."

"You sure are. Your job is to hold it until I'm ready." He smoothed her hair away from her face. "Dillon, can you help me with the lights?"

"Sure, Daddy."

"Do you mind if I play Christmas music? It might help you get in the holiday spirit."

"Uh—um." He stuttered and shuffled his feet. Was he ready for all the Holly Jolly?

Halo stepped forward and whispered. "This holiday has great potential for being different. Look who got stranded in a snowstorm in front of your house. I can help." She did a double thumb point at herself and smiled. "You're doing it for them. In the process you might as well have fun."

He blew out a noisy huff. "Jury's out on me." His chin jutted out and his body stiffened.

"Don't be so sure. There's still hope."

He wanted to believe her. "I'll do anything for my children." He tilted his head to the side and pursed his lips. "Where's your family for the holiday?"

Quicker than a rabbit, Halo turned and darted to the kitchen.

Presley caught up, touching her arm with the back of his hand, his voice soft. "Talk to me."

* * *

HER HAND CUPPED her mouth and Halo fought for words. "I'm a sentimental wreck, but I trust you."

"It's okay. Breathe." He gave a heavy nod.

"I lost my parents when I was almost four." Her chin quivered, and she crumpled as she tried to hold it together. "After their death, my great-aunt raised me, but she passed around the holidays. I spent the rest of my youth in the foster care system. I've been on my own most of my life."

Presley touched her forearm. "I'm sorry. So much loss, and you were so young." His tone soothing, "Sounds like we both know too much about loss and being alone."

His words gave her pause; an ugly cry was about to explode. "Thank you. It's been a while since I've told anyone about my past. I'm glad it was you I'm stranded with."

"Me too. Come join us." He waved her on.

"You should make new traditions with your family, not with a stranger."

He scratched his head and retreated into the other room but turned his gaze. "This has been...an unexpected surprise. You are no stranger, Halo Wrightway. We seem to have a lot in common."

* * *

PRESLEY HANDED HER AN ORNAMENT. "I saved one for you."

Halo declined as she watched from afar.

"No excuses. It's tradition. Everyone puts an ornament on the tree. Besides, Suzi is waiting to put the star on the top."

"Come on, Miss Halo, we saved our favorite one for you. It's an angel. See the halo? Just like your name."

She moved forward, carefully grasping the tiny white and gold ornament and placed it on the tree. Presley lifted Suzi as she placed the star on the treetop.

"Can we watch Rudolf? Please?" she asked as Presley lowered her to the floor.

"Yes, you can," he said, rolling his eyes.

Dillon walked over to Halo and tugged on her shirt. "Will you watch it with us? I'm afraid of the Bumble."

She kneeled. "You bet! It's my favorite." She tapped him on the nose. "Don't tell anyone, but I think the Bumble's teeth are scary."

Halo hoped she could hold it together with no waterworks when all the reindeer didn't let Rudolf play any reindeer games.

* * *

PRESLEY COULDN'T STOP STARING at Halo during the movie. Suzi and Dillon were sitting next to her like two bookends, and Champ had laid his head on one of her feet. She twisted her hair around her finger and bounced her knee up and down. The way she lip-synced to the music was cute, but when she tried to hide her tear-filled eyes, he came undone. When the kids belted out the Rudolf tune, she sang with them. He wanted to join in.

After they had tucked the kids into bed, Presley poured them both a glass of wine. They ended up talking for hours by Christmas tree lights. Halo had turned the holiday completely around for him, and Presley found himself wishing for more.

What am I thinking? Why would a single woman want to waste her time with a ready-made family and a widower with baggage?

But maybe he could wish for a while.

* * *

THE GARAGE CALLED EARLY the next morning while they were making pancakes. There was a wry twist to Presley's lips when he told Halo, "Appears you'll be spending the next several days here at Casa DeVry." He shrugged his shoulders. "Travel not advised. A bigger storm front is rolling through."

The doorbell rang just then, and Champ almost knocked Presley over as he dashed to the front door. Outside was a red and green striped Christmas box with a cut-out on the top.

"What the…?" Presley locked his arms around Champ before the dog darted out, but a tremendous gust of wind blew the door open and snow hit him in the face. He wrestled the dog and the box inside, then slammed the door shut. Champ bounded forward to get to the contents, barking, sniffing, and clawing. "Come on fella, relax."

"Daddy, maybe Santa came early?" Suzi asked.

"Look, there's a note," Dillon shouted.

Merry Christmas. Please give us a wonderful home. Love, Mavis and Mabel

P.S. Give Halo our best.

"Open it," Suzi squealed.

The box shifted, and Champ pounced on it.

Halo stepped closer. "Shhh… listen. I hear something."

They all stilled when meowing came from the box. Presley fell backward. Halo knelt and slowly opened the box.

That's when everything went at warp speed. Two black and white kittens scurried out of the box and Champ whizzed after them. One kitten zoomed behind the tree, fur raised and hissing, and the other scurried up the Christmas tree, followed by Champ.

The tree swayed and toppled over, all the ornaments scattering across the floor. Champ got tangled up in the lights and dragged everything through the living room with a kitten in tow.

Halo yanked at the end of the lights and halted a garland-wrapped Champ in the middle of his mass destruction.

One kitten high jumped onto the back of the couch, followed by the children and Halo. "Kids, stay where you are! You don't want to get cut by the broken bulbs," Presley rumbled as he took the dog by the collar and shooed him into his kennel, then limped off to the kitchen, holding his lower back.

The smoke alarm blared. Halo covered the kids' ears.

Smoke billowed in the air. Presley flicked off the gas burner and rammed the broom at the alarm and opened the back door to the seasonal porch. He tossed the spatula he had been using on the pancakes in the air. "Merry frickin' Christmas."

* * *

"WHERE'S DADDY?" Dillon asked.

Halo released her grip on the children. "He's fine. Stay here. I'll go find him." She handed the children the kittens.

She found Presley pacing the back porch. "There you are. I thought you had run away from home."

His hands clutched his hair. "I probably should have! This has been a disaster."

"How so?"

Bringing a shaky hand to his forehead, he mumbled, "Kittens, carnage, burned pancakes."

"It could have been worse. There was no fire, and you still have electricity," she said with a smirk.

"All I wanted to do was give the kids the best Christmas. I spent half the day yesterday getting everything imaginable for them. Look at all of this stuff." He pointed through the master bedroom window to the mountain of gifts, shopping bags, and wrapping paper piled on the bed. "Christmas threw up in there. And I think the bomb cyclone hit the living room."

Halo peered through the window, noticing a faint whiff of smoke from the kitchen when she leaned towards the house. The Christmas mountain was full of dolls, toys, and stuffed animals.

"That's a lot of gifts."

"You haven't seen everything. It's in every hidey-hole imaginable."

"Hm. I see. Come on inside." She closed the door and pulled a chair out from the kitchen table. "Sit. Don't move. I'll clean up." She placed her hands on his shoulders, forcing him into the chair, then scurried to the other room with a garbage can and dustpan. In her best Terminator voice, she called, "I'll be back," over her shoulder.

* * *

"Do you have anything we can add to this coffee? I don't mean creamer."

He pointed. "In the refrigerator, top right. Stronger stuff is in the upper cupboard."

"We can do shots later if this doesn't help." She filled the mugs with coffee and Irish cream, then sat next to him. "Okay. Just breathe."

He rubbed his eyes and inhaled deep, his shoulders relaxing. "When Abby got ill, someone told me to smile, because things could get worse. Well, they did. She wasn't supposed to get pregnant with Suzi. She got worse after, then she died."

"You're waiting for something to get worse?"

"Yes. Like a sledgehammer to the pie-hole. I've stuck my head in the sand for years, not feeling anything outside of these kids. It hit me hard on a call lately, so my boss forced me to take a sabbatical."

"Have you ever thought that all of this is creating a much-needed distraction?"

"It's working."

The kids' laughter echoed from the other room. She extended her hand. "Follow me. I want to show you something." Hitching her thumb, she asked, "What do you see?"

He shifted his gaze and glanced at the children. "I don't..."

"I see your two beautiful babies laughing and having fun. You're responsible for that." She ran a soothing hand across his back. "You don't have to buy them presents. All you need to do is love them, give them your time, teach them to be good humans, and give them a safe place to land."

He stood a little taller, savoring the moment as pride and satisfaction filled him. He was a good father and never fell short on the love he had for his littles.

"Look at them. They are having so much fun with a string and two fur babies. They're oblivious to everything else." Halo scrunched her nose and bumped against Presley. "I never had those. I spent most of my life praying for the simplest things. A sibling, a home, a father."

Presley slapped his forehead, crinkling his eyes tight and huffing out a breath. "How insensitive of me. I'm an asshat. Forgive me."

Halo leaned into him. "It's my journey. I'm not ashamed." She raised a hand to his cheek, her expression soft. "Stop trying to save the world. Don't try to be so perfect, because you will just fall."

* * *

"Thank you for the gentle reminder."

"I used a huge sledgehammer." She spread her arms wide.

"How did you get so wise?"

"Life." She tapped her temple. "I've had a lot of practice."

"Halo, you slid into our life when we needed you most. Thank you."

"Nice pun. Ha." She gave him a thumbs up. "My pleasure."

"You like that?" he said with a grin.

The children squealed and ran to them.

"Daddy, look what we found. What is it?" Suzi asked.

"Mistletoe," he answered, a glimmer of an idea forming in his mind.

"What's it for?" Dillon asked, his curious eyes squinting as he examined the plastic spray of leaves.

Presley bent forward, plucking the decoration from his son's hand and raising it above Halo's head. He looked into her eyes and saw the smile forming there, so he kissed her.

"It's for kissing? Gross, Daddy. Ew...."

HALO'S HEART rapped like a piston under her breastbone. She could feel the fire in her cheeks as a flush spread across them when Presley leaned in to kiss her. The way his intense gaze pierced her resolve undid her composure, and he was heading in for one more on the smacker. All the internal bells and whistles were chiming, throwing her system into a puddle of goo. Her brain was in literal haywire. Mush. Yabba-dabba-dude is right! How could this father of two she had only met have such an effect on her?

In a good way. Not complaining.

Her lashes fluttered and she wet her lips, giving them a proper *'kiss me silly, you fool'* pucker. She nervously awaited his next move as he dangled the mistletoe over her head once again. *Hurry up, handsome!* His lips appeared molten hot, a literal four-alarm blaze. *Or is that me?*

The children were practically glued to her and their father. Champ's cold nose nudged her hand to get in the mix. The children's inquisitive eyes were wide as saucers and the toothless grins stretched across their faces waiting in awe and wonderment over what was about to transpire. *Guess we all are.*

Her system quaked with anticipation; warmth surrounded her. *Keep it together.* All of this was foreign: one moment she wanted to flee so she wouldn't get disappointed, the next hang on tight. She'd wished for this most of her life. Since she had first walked into their house, she was different. The loneliness that once echoed deep in her soul was changing into an overflowing pool of solidarity. Whether it was in her imagination or not, she belonged somewhere. She mattered.

Temporary, considering the weather. Would they have met, or would she ever be here otherwise? *I know the answer. Probably never.*

Emotion seeped from every pore as goosebumps prickled her skin. Presley's breath warmed her skin and soothed her nerves. What she saw in his eyes was about to unglue every emotion she held inside. Every cell in her body recognized, unequivocally, she was safe. This powerful man filled gaps and crevices she thought would never heal. The children gave her hope for a future, and all of it was wrapped up in a snowstorm of tinsel and chaos.

Presley inched closer, and she stood on her tippy toes as he ran his nose against her and closed his eyes. *Here it comes... the moment.*

My moment.

One second, they were almost lip-locked, the next, a shadow came over his face. He hissed and bounced on one leg. Presley nearly fell back flat onto the kitchen table. The sound grated as he groaned. A black and white kitten clawed its way up his leg, followed by the other almost identical one. His eyes were scrunched closed, and he squirmed and yelped in visible pain.

"You're drawing blood. I'm not a tree. That's gonna leave a mark, you critters."

Somehow, one of the dynamic duo ended up on his shoulder and the other yowled, hanging on to one of his belt loops for dear life. He groaned as each claw penetrated his skin.

A flash of movement caught her eye. The horse-sized dog was in pounce posture, his back end swaying this way and that, then his whimpering shifted to low, pitiful grunts. The kittens appeared to be enjoying antagonizing him as much Champ the wonder dog was. He bounded forward, barely able to contain himself as his nails slid and scored the kitchen floor. *Poor Champ.* Presley whirled, his hips gyrating round and round as if he was in a hula-hoop competition.

HALO BIT at her top lip, warding off a fit of laughter, then grabbed Suzi and swung her around, just missing the dog pile on top of Presley. Dillon giggled and tried to wrestle the dog away as his father held up two kittens like a couple of boxing gloves and scooted away. Beads of sweat covered his forehead, and his hair was in disarray. Little pinpricks of crimson dotted his grey thermal shirt where the kittens had drawn blood. His blue eyes gleamed in disapproval, scanning the area, and he jumped into action. Halo sensed he was a quick thinker, razor sharp, calculated. He assessed his next move with measure and zero trepidation. He was trained to act fast and fast he was.

Halo inched away and hid around the doorway with Suzi. She covered her mouth, willing her pulse to slow its roll. The little girl clung to her leg. "It's okay, sweetie your daddy is fine, and the kittens are just scared. Halo bit at her lip hard trying to stop another fit of laughter. I'm sure if you give the kittens a little more time, they'll settle in with Champ and make them-selves at home" She had a kinship with Presley's youngest already. Both losing their mothers at an early age formed them in a club neither would have preferred. Dillon too.

"Like you did, right, Halo? We just met and now it's like we've known you a long time," the little girl probed with her cherub face and big doe eyes.

"You're right. I guess I did. How did you get so smart, anyway?" She squeezed Suzi on the cheek and ran her hand over her static-laden hair. How could things change so fast? One minute she was giving Presley the googly stare and the next…animal apocalypse. She stole another look at Presley, who was standing there with a dog wrapped around him and two hair-raised kittens hissing the light fantastic.

This was the best holiday eveerrr.

"That didn't exactly go the way I had hoped." Presley wiped the sweat off his brow with the sleeve of his shirt, dangling the furballs in his grasp. "You sure you're still on board with being stuck here? There's never a dull moment." He gave her a half smile.

"Absolutely. I pride myself on handling most situations only a few things give me the heebie-jeebies. I'm sure it's more difficult on you than it is on me and I'm quite enjoying the show." Halo looked out the foggy window to the blinding white out and ran her hands over her arms. "Brrr. It looks cold out there. I think I'll stay put."

"Good. Me too, but I'm maimed." He snickered. "Even if I'm your last option because there's a blizzard."

Halo held up her hands. "Trust me. Not complaining a bit."

Presley winked and said, "Now that we have this matter settled, where were we?" He stepped closer with the two kittens, eyeballing Champ. "No funny business, fella." The big dog wagged his tail, then hunkered down with his head on the floor and whimpered. Dillon picked up the mistletoe and dangled it above his head, darting forward, cutting his father off at the pass. "My turn, Miss Halo!" he shouted, followed by a laugh.

"Champ is next," he said as he leaned closer with protruding duck-like lips.

Halo knelt on the floor in front of the freckled-nosed little boy. "How could I resist?" She swept the hair off the boy's forehead. Erasing the distance, she kissed him on the cheek, then another. He jumped around the room, giggling. "Now Champ." He tugged on the mammoth dog's collar. Halo wrapped her arms around the retriever's neck, kissing him on top of the head. His tail revved up a tempo and Champ gave her a lick of his tongue. "Thanks for wetting my whistle." Halo grimaced, wiping her face.

"Me, me, me," Suzi squealed. She snatched the plastic thing from her brother's hand and wiggled it above her head. "My turn."

"Are you sure you want to kiss me after the dog?"

"He doesn't have cooties, Miss Halo. I kiss him all the time." Suzi hugged her tight, almost choking her. She gasped for air as the girl gave her a smack on the lips. Halo laughed and searched Presley's demeanor during their exchange. His eyes were glassy as she caught a glint of moisture in his gorgeous eyes.

* * *

OVERCOME BY SENTIMENT, Presley struggled to swallow the gigantic boulder lodged in his throat. He held the kittens to his chest as they purred, concentrating on stroking their whiskers and soft fur, warding off a potential assault on his ticker. He couldn't remember the last time he was filled with so much emotion, other than grief. *Today is a good day.*

He missed Abby. He spun the wedding ring around his finger, pulling it on and off. His wife had been gone just over three years, and he was so lonely for adult companionship. He squeezed and flexed his hand, inspecting the ring. He missed a partnership. *So damn lonely.* Halo stirred something he thought he'd never feel again.

Hope.

His shoulders relaxed as he wiped his nose, dodging another threat of a Hallmark moment. *Nothing like swinging in the totally opposite direction on the sap scale. Seriously? What's gotten into you, dude?*

He exited the kitchen, putting the kittens in Champ's carrier, cocooning them in a heavy fleece throw. Maybe if he was lucky, they'd take a siesta. Retreating seconds later without the kittens, he snatched several coloring books and two boxes of crayons from a nearby shelf with renewed anticipation. "Okay, kiddos, I think we need to give our guest a minute from the crazy train. Who wants to color?" He pulled a chair out and took Halo's hand in his. "Let's give this another go." He filled her cup with a little more coffee. "I bet you're hungry." He tugged at his shirt.

Halo ran her fingers down the silver chain of her locket and cleared her throat. "Yes. Very."

He snapped his fingers together repeatedly. "Do you like chocolate chip pancakes?" Presley plodded across the kitchen, emptied a box of pancake mix into a bowl, then measured the water.

"You sure I can't help?" Halo said as she readjusted herself in the chair.

"Nope, this time I swear I got this." He smiled and gave her a thumbs up. "I need to repay the debt. The way things are looking, my list is getting longer."

"Hasn't it been your treat?" Halo's cheeks reddened, and she looked at her locket again. "I'm not sure who's in debt to whom. You've opened your home to a stranger during the holidays, clothed me, and assaulted my senses with an abundance of Christmas joy. My glass is running over and it's not even Christmas yet."

"You're not a stranger anymore. Right, Miss Halo?" Suzi asked.

"My mistake. I forgot." She smiled and swooshed a stray hair from her face. "It's like we've known each other forever."

"Like family." The little girl hummed as she colored, her eyes never once leaving the page.

Presley inspected his precious little girl and gazed back at Halo. Waves rippled through his gut.

"Remember what I do for a living? It's my oath to aid and protect those in need. I just didn't think you would come to our rescue. This had all the potential of being a cross between Animal House and Christmas with the Kranks, if you hadn't saved the day." He set the batter-filled red plastic bowl on the counter and crossed the kitchen. Presley lifted Halo's hand and kissed the top of it. "Thank you for choosing my street to get stranded on."

"You can thank my overtime hours delivering food to your neighbors."

Still holding her hand, towering over her, Presley said, "I'll have to donate more to the Dinners for Seniors and thank them properly for the early Christmas gift." He waggled his eyebrows and gave her a wry smile. *A woman who wears her heart on her sleeve.* Presley inspected the rosy color of her cheeks. He released her hand and fiddled with the button on his shirt. "Except for the kitten part."

Uh, hum. Halo cleared her throat and waved a hand at her face. "Is it getting warm in here?"

"I'm fine, Miss Halo."

Her eyes darted to Dillon, who was engrossed in his coloring book.

"I think I'll go splash my face. Yes, hot." She bolted out of her chair and hurried to the restroom.

* * *

Butterflies danced in her stomach. "Geez, you swoony thing. Keep it together. Mr. Handsome Firefighter, doting father of two, is so out of your league." Her eyes widened in embarrassment as she pressed her hands to her blotchy reflection. *So not in your league, toots.*

Halo's ears perked up at a tap on the door. Presley peeked his head in.

"Are you feeling okay?"

She hurled herself forward and kissed him on the lips. Knee deep in the feelings swirling round and around, she was light-headed. Halo wasn't just kissing Presley; he was kissing her back and *whoa*, in a toe-curling hubba-hubba kind of way. His tongue dipped between the seam of her lips. Her chest felt like it might explode. Warmth spread up her arms and into her chest as she caressed the back of his neck, threading her fingers through his hair. His kiss went deeper, more urgent. One minute she wanted to gasp for air, the next drink him in. Strong protective arms wrapped around her, hands stroked the flesh along her back, deft fingers swirling and littering goosebumps on top of goosebumps. She drew a line along his chiseled jaw, then swept the pads of her fingers along his corded neck.

"Daddy, we're hungry," Dillon bellowed from the other room. "When are we eating?"

Presley's breathing was ragged as he sucked air into his lungs. His chest heaved as he held her steadfast. *Wish I could say the same.* Her knees were about to give underneath her. *Feet don't fail me now, feet don't fail me now.*

His sweet breath lingered just above her swollen lips. "My heart is frickin' outside of my chest right now." He put a fist to his mouth and exhaled. "I kid you not." He closed his eyes and blew out another breath. "Just a minute," he rasped towards Dillon. "Crap! Daddy duty calls," he said to her in a low growl, his gaze intense. "But..." He hesitated, then went into another earth-wobbling kiss. This time he moaned, pressing his forehead to hers. "I should go." He didn't move.

Halo held a finger to her lips, still feeling the sensation of the knee-knocking encounter.

He whistled. "That kiss… whoa…"

"I—I shouldn't have." Halo stood stiff and backed away. "I'm not that kind of girl to be so forward." Her heart stumbled before finding its rhythm once again.

He pulled her closer. "You're not getting away that easily. Yes, you should have, and I'd like to revisit it a little later." He kissed her again. "You're a respectable woman, Halo. No boundaries were crossed." They jumped, this time to Suzi whimpering from behind as she tugged on Presley's shirt. "Daddy, I want chocolate pancakes, please. Can you make a smiley?"

He spun around and ran his hand over the top of his little girls' flyaway strands. "Anything for my bestest girl." Glancing over his shoulder, Presley whispered, "Don't you ever regret that kiss. I won't." Meaningful eyes probed her intently.

She nodded and willed herself to make a legible sentence. Gulping hard, she got a word or two out.

"Be—uh—a moment," Halo said as she closed the bathroom door.

Once solo, she leaned against the wall and scrubbed her face. "What have you done now?" She stepped to the mirror and saw her cheeks were a deeper scarlet then before, her lips pink and plump. She ran the top of her finger over them, reliving the sensation of his full lips upon hers. *Wowza!*

Halo turned on the faucet and soaked a washcloth with cold water, blotting her face and chest. Anything to cool off. *Cold shower anyone?* "Seriously. What did you do? And when in the tarnation did you get so daring?" she whispered to no one, puffing out a breath to blow her bangs off her face.

That man dills my pickle.

A snicker escaped, lifting the corners of her mouth. *Brazen hussy.* Knowing full well she was not in the slightest, she also knew there was no holding back from this day forward on what or who she wanted. She said a silent prayer to the universe. Knowing there was something cosmic in the works that had landed her here with Presley and his sweet family. *Y'all, I believe there is Christmas magic in the works.*

Memories of her Great Auntie flooded in, and Halo remembered her promise to fight for what she wanted, even if she assumed there was no hope.

Always the visionary... Great Auntie's words resonated as clear as the locket she wore around her neck. Halo could still hear her say, *one day my child, a knight in shining armor will come upon you when you least expect it, but you must know who you are and what you want. Until then, you won't be ready. People will come and go in your life until the right one sticks. They will be as lost as you once were, but you will guide him forward and he will be worthy of the love you have in your heart. You will feel it in every fiber of your being that he is the one. He will give you everything you had hoped for. He will be your destiny.*

Auntie's words were as present today as they were years ago. *My sweet Halo, your road will not be an easy one, but you are meant to shine, so dazzle your hero and make an old lady happy. Your mother, father, and I will be watching over you, and we can't wait to see it all unfold*

Halo waved her hands to ward off sentimental overload and a full-blown blubber fest. She peered into her reflection. *Should I dare hope?*

Nothing in her life ever panned out, but one day it would be her turn. *Is this what Auntie spoke of?*

Halo pulled her shoulders back and made her way to the kitchen. She eyed the children, who wore more of the chocolate on their faces than in their bellies. Halo stood beside Presley, who was at the counter working with strategic intent on their own plates. She peered onto the plate to see blueberry eyes, chocolate smiley faces, a strawberry nose and whipped cream hair on the award-winning pancakes.

"Talented."

He snickered. "I have endless abilities in fun, kid friendly foods. Don't tell anyone because my reputation at the fire station would be ruined. You should see what I do to make them eat their veggies."

She kicked her head back and laughed. "Your secret is safe with me. What kind of person would I be if I tattled on the very person who saved me from freezing to death and is feeding me such a prized pancake specimen?" She crinkled her nose and elbowed Presley. "Especially on Christmas Eve morning."

Presley was her knight in shining armor. This big brute of a firefighter was a grumpy bear at first but had a soft spot. He was the entire package.

"Let's eat. Sorry about the kids; they couldn't wait another minute. They said they were starving to death." He chuckled.

"They look to be a suffering duo. I'm sure they also walked barefoot for miles in a blizzard to school." She rolled her eyes. "You tyrants."

"Right." Presley pulled out a chair for halo and took the seat beside her. "Enjoy your one-of-a-kind Devry happy meal." He tipped his fork against hers and passed her the syrup after he slathered his own.

"I can't wait." She dipped her finger in the whipped cream and put it in her mouth, passing on the syrup. Halo cut her pancake in half, going straight for the melted chocolate chips. Taking a bite, she closed her eyes and moaned. "Best food faced happy meal I've ever had."

* * *

Presley was transfixed by Halo. He had a difficult time concentrating after their kiss, and his appetite was not for the food. His body ached with longing. *You are mesmerizing.* She was so animated and easy to be around. He felt a lightness, a burden eased. Good thing she happened upon them. Life was sizing up with her in the vicinity. Things were on the upswing, indeed. He inched his hand closer to hers and leaned in, whispering in her ear. "Do you think I could recruit your help today?"

"Sure thing. I must earn my room and board."

"Remember the pile of stuff?" He jerked his head toward the seasonal porch.

She nudged him. "You mean Mount Everest?" She took another bite of her pancake.

He smirked. "There's truth to those words. I need a wing-woman." He had a difficult time focusing.

Halo wiped her mouth with a napkin. "Happy to oblige. This is so exciting!" she whispered in his ear, glancing at the children.

"Daddy, why are you whispering?" Dillon asked.

"It's a Christmas secret."

"What? No fair."

"No fair, Daddy," Suzi mimicked.

"I was talking to Halo about what wonderful children you have been."

"Yes, your father told me he heard from an excellent source that you're not on the naughty list."

"Santa Claus told you that?" Suzi's eyes widened as she held a crayon midair.

"He might have, but there's still another day to be for certain."

Dillon belted out a tune. "He knows if you've been bad or good, so we better be good or else..."

Suzi sang her own interesting rendition of the song along with Dillon. Presley stood from his seat, grabbing the plates and setting them in the sink. "Time to clean up. We have lots to do today." He helped Suzi from her booster seat.

Halo jumped up. "You three go on and get going. I got this handled."

"You don't have to do that."

"Oh yes I do, I can get it done lickity-split." She anchored a hand on her hip. "Scoot, scram, and all that jazz," she said, waving them out of the room.

Presley looked over his should and gave her a wink. He nudged the kiddos in their rooms. "Pick out what you want to wear today. You first, Dillon." He tapped his son on his bottom.

"Daddy, do I have to change?"

"Yes, you do. I think you're wearing more of your food than you ate."

The boy lifted his shirt and pushed out his tummy. "I think my belly is happy."

"Good! You want to grow big and strong."

"Just like you." Dillon lifted his arms and flexed.

"It's just as important to strengthen your mind as it is to get fit." He tapped his son's temple.

"I'm already smart, so smart I know I'm wearing my Superman cape again today."

Presley ran a hand over the silky fabric. "You can wear your cape today, but you must change. You don't want Miss Halo to think we're smelly, do you?"

"She likes us. I don't think she will care because she really likes you." The boy climbed onto his bed and jumped up and down.

"Why do you say that?" Presley cocked his head and listened carefully.

"Because when you were going to smooch her, she moved her lashes all funny. I've seen that on TV."

He covered his eyes. "What shows are you watching?"

The boy squealed and jumped off the bed and ran to his dresser, yanking open a drawer. "Can we stay in our jammies all day?"

"I suppose so. It's too cold to go outside and we can wear whatever we like."

"I'll wear my blue Superman pj's to match my cape." He bounced around with excitement. "I'm a superhero."

"Perfect, son. Stop stalling for a second. Let's get you in the shower so we can get your chocolate mustache off. I think you have whipped cream in your hair."

The boy got a peek of his face in the mirror over his dresser and screamed, "I'm a man just like you. I'm all growded up."

"Better not grow up so fast." *Where have the years gone?* He tapped at the face of his watch. "You have fifteen minutes, then I'm coming to look for you. Your sister is probably stuck to a surface somewhere."

"Don't worry, I'll hurry. Santa is watching. I don't want to be on the naughty list."

"You got that right." Presley nudged his son out of the room and down the hall to Suzi's room, but she wasn't there. He entered the kitchen and caught sight of Halo washing the last of the dishes with Suzi standing on a chair at her side. Their heads were together, deeply immersed in their conversation.

He leaned against the doorway, crossing an ankle over another, relishing the exchange. Minutes passed, so he cleared his throat. He startled the helper and her lady, who ended up slinging water across the floor.

Halo clutched the embroidered kitchen towel to her chest, apparently stunned. Suzi wasn't fazed. "You scared the wits out of me."

"Sorry. I didn't mean to spook you." Presley pinched his lips in an attempt not to laugh.

Halo played it off. "Be careful, Suzi. I'll help you down. I don't want you to slip on the water." She eased the girl to the floor and bent down, putting a finger over her mouth, then poking her in the belly. "Shhh. Remember, it's a secret." She guided the little girl to her father.

"Daddy, Miss Halo let me help with the dishes."

Halo covered her mouth and giggled. "Yes, and I don't think I could've managed without her. We might have given her a bath and cleaned the floor too."

"Really?" He gauged the water-logged floor and her clothes. "That's great, sweetie. Why don't you go pick out what you want to wear today. Dillon is wearing his pjs. You can too if you like."

Suzi took off to her room, shouting, "Yippee, skippy."

"Who knew they'd be so excited about sleepwear? Hey, don't worry about the floor. It needs a once over." He grabbed the mop and bucket and began clean up.

Halo whipped around at the sound of shutters banging against the window frame. The wind whined and rustled through the trees.

"I better get more firewood and stoke the fire; it's supposed to get really cold tonight. You can hear the wind picking up."

"Is this normal? You can't see a thing out there."

Presley continued running the mop over the saturated floor, squeezing the excess water into the bucket. "It is here. Every now and then, we get a doozy like this one."

Halo shivered. "I guess be careful what you wish for. I wanted a white Christmas because I never had one in the South."

"So, it's all your fault?" he razzed. "I guess the Midwest welcomed you proper."

"Apparently. I wouldn't have been prepared at all in my apartment and my car was not snow ready and I shouldn't have driven in this weather. I swan dived into an abyss of poor decisions."

"Not all. You are safe here and warm. Growing up here, we always expect the unexpected." Presley tilted his head to one side, studying the expression on her face. "Truly unexpected in the best possible way." His fingers tingled as they skimmed over her soft skin. "I better go check on the kids. They are being terribly quiet. Could be trouble."

Halo listened closely, then took the mop from his grip. "Might be a good idea."

Presley tiptoed down the hallway and into his daughter's room. She was dressed up in a pink boa and a princess crown, sipping on a plastic cup of tea. She had stripped all her dolls' dresses; one kitten wore a black and white checkered outfit and squirmed around, attacking a red ribbon Suzi had wrapped around its head. The other kitten was in a pink baby onesie, sound asleep on its back.

How did the kittens get out of Champ's carrier? He inched away, careful not to disturb, and grabbed his phone from his back pocket, taking a few shots to document the moment. He snuck down the hall to Dillon's room, where he was reading one of his favorite books and petting Champ. His heart filled exponentially. His kids were his life. Maybe this time home was a sign. He needed to get it in check before he went back to work. Lives and the guys at the firehouse depended on him, but so did his kids. Why had he let things get so bad? And why did he not see it before?

He retreated from his son's room and called his cousin Lauren to check in on her.

"Hey, there. I thought I'd call and make sure everything's okay." He paced the hallway.

"All cozy."

"Do you need me to trudge over and shovel for you?"

"Don't you dare. Stay put; we are golden. How are the kids?"

"They're great." Presley whipped around to see Dillon standing in his doorway. "Hey pal."

"Daddy, is that Leelee?"

Presley nodded.

Dillon reached up. "Can I talk to her?"

"Sure. Hey, Dillon wants to talk to you."

"Hi Leelee. Miss you. Guess what?" Dillon blurted out. "We've had company for a few days…"

"Dillon, wait!" Presley tried to get him to stop, but it was too late.

"She's real pretty and I think Daddy really likes her."

Presley locked his teeth tight. "Dillon, shhhh…" He turned around as the floorboard creaked and Halo froze. Her cheeks turned bright red.

"I think she really likes Daddy too, because she gets all red when she looks at him, like she is right now."

"Enough. Give me the phone back. Thanks for spilling the beans, pal." He rolled his eyes and shook his head, then put the phone to his ear and mouthed "Sorry," to Halo.

"I'm back." Presley ran a hand through his hair.

"Do tell…" he heard on the other end of the line.

"Dillon and his big mouth. I'm sure you have a ton of questions, but here's the gist of it all. A couple of days ago, a woman delivered food to the neighbors when the storm started and her car got stuck. The battery died. You know how the town rolls up the welcome mat and shuts the lights off?" He paused, listening to his cousin, only to laugh. "Come on, no, she isn't a serial killer or an escapee from the looney-bin." Presley lumbered back and forth across the living room. He thought maybe if he walked faster, the conversation would end before he hit the point of no return for yet another embarrassing episode. "She's delivering food for seniors until after the holidays, then she substitutes for Miss Penelope. Are you up to speed?"

"Got it. Is she the pretty blonde in town everyone has been talking about for the past month?" his cousin drilled. "The entire town is in the know."

"Where have I been? Under a rock?" he questioned.

"In a matter of speaking, for longer than you should have been."

"Yes, that would be the one. She's standing right here. Do

you want to talk to her? Or I can send you her bio." Presley put a hand over his mouth and laughed. He pressed the phone closer to his ear.

"Let me ask you this. I sense an entire new attitude going on here. Does this person have anything to do with it?" Lauren inquired.

Presley's gaze darted to Halo. "I plead the fifth. Nunaya business. Love ya, gotta go." He ended the call and ruffed up Dillon's hair. "Now you went and did it. We will be the talk of the town."

"I'm sorry, Daddy." Dillon's bottom lip protruded.

"No worries, pal, but it's not fair to our guest. Let them talk about me, I don't care, but she's new here." His mouth tightened in a grimace.

"I don't give a hoot. Let them chatter. If they have nothing better to do than be a bunch of Nosey Nellies, that's too bad." Halo anchored a fist on her hip and flipped a hand in the air. "I can handle it. No worries." Halo jerked her head to the side to get Presley to come hither, and he ambled forward. "It's okay, really, but thank you. Do you still need a wingman for your special project?"

"I do. Let me get the kiddos set up with a movie." He swung around. "Who wants to watch another Christmas show?"

"We do. We do," Suzi shouted. "Trolls Holiday."

"You've watched that hundreds of times. Are you sure?"

"Yes please, Daddy," Dillon exclaimed and clapped his hands in the air.

"*Trolls* it is." He plugged in the movie through the remote and turned up the volume. "Please, you two, behave. Daddy must take care of something, and I need you to watch your movie. If you're good, we can plan something fun later. If you need anything we will be in my room, but you must knock. Halo and I have a surprise for you two."

"Yay!"

Presley grabbed Halo's hand and tramped down the hall.

"Your kids are so stinking' cute. I want to gobble them up."

He whipped his gaze to her. His eyes flashed, every nerve aflame, his breath hissed out. "You're coming with me."

"The gift wrapping, right?" She blurted a laugh, barely able to keep up with his long-legged stride.

"That too, but I can't wait to have you all to myself." He opened the door to the master suite and shut it behind them, flipping the lock. He pressed Halo against the wall, running lazy circles along her neck. They were nose to nose. "Can I please kiss you? If I don't, I will suffer miserably," he said, nearly out of breath.

"I thought you'd never ask." She wrapped her arms around his neck and spun a lock of his hair around her finger. "But should we?"

"The kids will knock. I know we haven't known one another long, but I feel as if we were destined to be right here, right now. I'm not sure about anything but this. You're a godsend." He rested his head against hers. "It's been so long since I felt anything." Presley struggled to regain his words. He had so much he wanted to say. He inched back, tracing her lips with the tip of his finger. "My heart has ached for so long and I never thought it was ever possible to feel this way again. You graced us with your presence, and it feels natural. Does that even make sense, or am I just a rambling fool?"

He backed away further and held up his hands. "It's not fair to you. I apologize if I'm coming on too strong. I swear I'm not a creeper. Here you are, stranded in my home, and you can't go anywhere." He pivoted to turn away, and Halo caressed his hand.

"I'm not fearful of you, Presley. I'm a grown woman, and I could probably kick your butt, anyway."

"Oh yeah?" He squinted his eyes and inspected her.

"I know self- defense. I've brought bigger men to their knees." She laughed. "A woman must protect herself." She gave a matter-of-fact nod. "Off topic. I know what you mean." She picked at imaginary lint on Presley's shirt. "Ending up here in front of your house was by far the best holiday I've had to date, in a weird unsuspected way. Even with my clunker getting stuck and the battery dying." She licked her lips and stammered for the right words. "You have been more than a gracious host when you even didn't have a choice. It was my bad, yet I'm blessed. It could have been fifty shades of awful."

He reached for her hand, lacing her fingers through his. "I couldn't leave a damsel in distress, could I? The moment you arrived, everything shifted. You know my story. It's been so many years that the holidays were locked and loaded with painful memories for the kids and me. You've brought us some peace." He ran a thumb over her creamy skin. "This is awkward, but you give me strength enough to make an ass out of myself." He lowered his chin and his shoulders slumped. "I'm afraid I'm going to blow it and scare you off."

She lifted his chin, her eyes filled with understanding. "How so?"

"I'd die if you felt threatened or uncomfortable. It hasn't exactly been a Norman Rockwell painting here. I mean...the dog, the tree, the kittens." He raked his hands through his hair. "I come with two kids. This is us, no filters. The kids are my life." He hoped if his words didn't resonate, she'd see what he felt in his eyes. *See me. I'm putting it out there.* "There's something undeniable about us, Halo,"

Halo stepped forward and cupped his cheek. "Trust me, I could tell you some stories. What I've seen here, in your home, is a dance in the park." Her lips curved in a smile. "I feel like this is a posh resort, and you've shown me nothing but kindness and respect."

"Come on." He rolled his eyes. "It's chaos."

She raised her hand and crossed her heart. "I'll tell you my take on this, but first... what about that kiss?"

Presley caged her against the wall and claimed her mouth. Her lips were soft as he remembered, and everything about her was so liberating. Nothing was forced; they fit. She tasted of the sweetest berries, and he relaxed into everything Halo encompassed. His issues evaporated, but she went to his mind's eye.

Presley ended the kiss but wanted so much more. Instead, he whisked her hair from her face and planted a kiss on one cheek, then the other, her forehead, and her delicate nose. "I'm sorry you had to go through any of the pain you did." He swallowed hard. He wanted to erase all her hurt if he could.

"Don't be. It is what it is, and it gives me extra flavor, having gone through it. Not all of it was bad. I choose to go onward and upward." Her chin lifted and jutted forward. "I can't be ashamed of my past, because it brought me here."

He leaned in and ran a finger along her jawline. "You're amazing."

"You're pretty darn special yourself, Presley Devry. Thank you for giving me a soft place to land."

"You haven't seen why I'm asking for your help yet. It's a big ask." He rubbed his eyes.

She stood a little straighter and pulled her shoulders back. "Try me. I'm not intimidated in the least."

He craned his neck toward his shopping disaster. This time she had a front-row looksee.

"I don't know where to start. I got a little carried away, and I'm not sure what I have."

"Wow!" Halo's eyes bulged out and her mouth hung open.

His brows knitted together. "Told you. I even recruited my cousin for a few things. I panicked when I heard the storm was coming. Usually it's not a thing, but this is my first holiday break with the kids. I admit it was way easier to keep it simple and go to Lauren's. But my counselor said it was imperative for me to climb out of my rut and try something different. She'd be proud. I think."

"What's done is done." Halo swooshed her hand in the air. "You're in luck, because I have mad organizational skills." She sorted through the bags. "Before we get knee deep in our knickers, we need vino."

"Good idea. I should check on the kids anyway. What kind of wine do you prefer?"

"You choose. I'm not picky."

"Back in a flash." He leaned in and gave her another kiss on the cheek.

* * *

"GET that kiss out of your noggin' and focus." She snapped her fingers in front of her face. *Hello, I said focus.* Halo emptied the contents out of one bag, then another. She was not lucky in life, but these kids were. *If you've never had it, you won't miss it. Don't wish for things and you'll never be disappointed.* She had all she needed: a roof over her head, food, an education she had fought for, and a job for the future. So much more than she ever had. Christmas was about so much more than the commercialization.

Presley knocked on the door. "It's me," he whispered.

Halo opened the door. He had a bag of cheese popcorn in his mouth and two glasses of Sparkling Rosé. She grabbed the bag from his lips. "There's more." He spun around. "I ran out of hands."

It was very possible she was distracted by his backside, but she managed to pull a pack of peanut butter crackers and a dark chocolate bar from the pocket of his snug jeans.

His eyes crinkled, and he smirked. "It's the best I could do. I figured we needed rations."

Halo's heart warmed. "Absolutely perfect."

"So, any thoughts?" Presley handed her a glass of wine. "I chose a sweeter Moscato Rosé."

She sipped at the bubbly. "This is nice." She took another sip, and it tickled her nose as she focused on the gift mountain in front of them. "Yes, you may have overshopped. From what I see already, you have duplicates. You can always return them." She tapped her chin. "One question. Did you leave anything for anyone else?"

He grimaced. "I panicked. This is only a small portion."

"Oh, dear." Her eyes widened.

"Let me get the rest of the haul. I'll be right back."

He snuck back in with a few more armloads of bags. "I'm not proud of myself. I just wanted to make this Christmas extra special. This isn't in my wheelhouse. Abby used to do all that stuff and after..." He hesitated. "My cousin took pity on me. She watches the kids when I'm on shift." He sat his glass aside and carried a small table over, then refilled the wine glasses and loaded the snacks.

"You being present for your children is all they need." Halo carried a few gifts she guessed were Suzi's to the floor and started wrapping. "You can see it on their faces." She pointed at the stack of Dillon's gifts. "Could you bring those here too?"

Presley set the gifts on the floor.

"Come sit." She patted the floor beside her.

He looked around and scratched his head. "Me?"

"Yes, you, get over here. This is a duo effort."

"Bossy. You know, if I get down there, you may have to help me up. That's a long way from where I'm standing."

"Deal! Come on, Gramps."

A smile tilted the corners of his mouth. "Open up." He threw a few kernels of popcorn in Halo's mouth. Presley kneeled on the floor, set the bag of popcorn aside and picked at his nail. "I guess I got used to it, but I started spiraling into a funk and I couldn't get out of it. When it affected my job, I was forced to get a reality check. The first sessions with a counselor were about grief, then I gave myself a swift kick." He fumbled with a gift, eyed the wrapping paper and cut it to size. "Guess I figured I was making up for lost time." He taped the paper haphazardly on a gift, placed the tag on it, and scribbled Dillon's name. "I wanted to share every childhood memory I remembered from growing up." He got up and brought several more gifts to the floor. "Then this storm put a damper on it." The more gifts he wrapped the worse they appeared. Halo inspected his attempt and gave a silent chuckle. He was so diligent.

"This is hard work." He blew out a painful sigh.

"It's not so bad, I love it." She hummed a Christmas melody. "Do you have any gift bags?"

Presley rummaged through another few mounds of his shopping haul and pulled out an assortment of different sized holiday bags. "You mean we can just shove the gifts in here?"

"Something like that. It's easier if wrapping isn't your thing."

Presley crossed the room in two strides. "Now we're talking." He grabbed handfuls of stuff and shoved it into the bags. "Done." He leaned against the wall proudly with his hands behind his head.

Halo scanned around. "I guess you are. The rest can be for Santa gifts and the stockings."

"Unless, I find more stuff, which is a strong possibility." He took a swig of his wine and reached for a pad and paper and handed it to Halo. "Here's my list of things I wanted to do with the kids."

"What are you, an overachiever? This is a huge list." She studied it and jumped up from where she was seated. "This is very ambitious, but amazing. I love it."

"Really? It's not too much?"

She held up a finger and thumb. "Maybe a little overzealous, but you have years to fulfill it all. Maybe when they're eighteen you might." She cupped her hand over her mouth and giggled. "I'd love to help. Let's sort everything, wrap a few things, then I'll take on part of your list."

"You'd do that?"

"In a heartbeat. Come on! Wrapping, baking, crafts, movies, snow angels, sledding, games, stockings—everything that screams Christmas holidays. This has all the potential of being the best holiday vacation ever for your children."

"I hope so. I know it's already looking up for me."

"Me too. Squeee! Let's make a plan." Halo tapped the pen against the pad of paper and inspected the list as excitement soared through her system. "Here's what I can do. I can bake, so leave that to me. I can see what you have and Google recipes" She jotted a note beside the task. We can hide their unwrapped Santa gifts and put the wrapped ones under the tree tonight. Then we can create a meal plan and set an agenda. We have today and tomorrow for Operation: Epic Christmas, but it can last as long as you want. Your house, your rules. Come on, partner."

HALO PREDICTED this was going to be the best Christmas for Presley and his kids. It already was for her, the only thing she had ever asked for through the years. Though Presley and the kids weren't her family, she wasn't alone as years past, and celebrating their yuletide joy was a close second.

She circled the items she planned to take on. "I'll be right back."

"Not so fast." He twirled her around. "Where do you think you are going?"

Her heart hammered in her chest from the close proximity, the attraction as strong as it had been since meeting him. She couldn't think when he was anywhere near her. She had to keep her head about her for the tasks. Her mouth worked soundlessly; the words unable to permeate her brain. Instead, they bounced around like rogue ping-pong balls. "Uhm—" She tripped over words that finally escaped. "Not sure. Oopsy, we need to hide the rest of the gifts first. I got ahead of myself."

"Thank you. Don't go please." A pained look marred his face. "We have so few stolen moments without the rugrats and a reprieve from the shenanigans. I like your company, if it isn't obvious already, and I just need to adult for a minute. It's been so long."

His eyes bored so deep into her soul, she went all weak in the knees. "Okay, it can wait. We have plenty of time for the rest." She threw the pad of paper onto the bed. "As long as… never mind." A spark pooled in her belly.

His breath hissed out, "Halo what you do to me. I can't help myself," he claimed her mouth.

* * *

PRESLEY CAUGHT a glimpse of an old photo of Abby. He ran a finger over the frame thinking of days long past. So much of his life had changed. Halo was so different from Abby. Neither looked like one another, and their personalities were unique to who they were. Abby had been bold and serious, whereas Halo held a whimsical quality, but had such depth when it came to people and their emotions. She could read him without judgement and had lived a thousand lifetimes in her youth. His heart ached for her loss, though she would not take his pity, and he had huge respect for her strength.

Halo was special, and he felt protective of her in ways he couldn't comprehend in the small amount of time they'd shared. She had an endearing quality about her that was kid-like, and her energy made him bubble with excitement.

"Hey you. Where did you go?"

Presley spun around.

"I'm sorry, I didn't mean to startle you. You're shaking, is everything okay?" Concern etched her expression, and she noticed what he was looking at.

He moved closer, what he saw in her eyes gave him strength. He swallowed his courage, letting the words slip through his lips. "I haven't felt this way in so long. I'm not sure I know what to do with the emotions flooding in. He looked over his shoulder at the photo. "Guilt has no place here."

"Guilt? It's okay if it does." Her head tilted to the side. "Come here, let's sit a moment." She directed him to the nearby bench. Her fingers trailed over his skin "Talk to me."

She soothed and patted his back. It had been eons since he had felt vulnerable and safeguarded. His armor broke free for the first time since Abby's loss. A tear slipped down his cheek and he wanted to weep in front of this woman he and his kids had bonded with as if she was family.

He pulled away, covering his eyes. "Dammit, what is this?"

"Look at me, Presley." She placed both hands on his cheeks. Her eyes were soft and comforting. "You've had to be strong for those beautiful babies. Christmas always gets me in the ticker too and I'm known to go *all boo hoo* if I see anyone else cry. I kid you not."

A tear slid down her cheek, and he wiped it away. "Look at us."

There would be no turning back for him. This moment they both shared their pain, but together united. A rebirth. A kinship. The universe was working overtime.

"You're so beautiful. He kissed her with all the pent-up passion he'd locked in. They held each other tight until there was a noise at the door. They jumped and moved away from one another. He could see kitty paws, four of them under the door, swatting as the kids giggled. The dog was cluck-barking. They gazed at one another.

"Back to mayhem." He shook his head and gave her a wry smile.

"I love the mayhem. It's invigorating." Halo plucked up the notepad and reached for the door.

"Wait." Presley stopped her from opening the door. He pulled her to his chest and kissed her again. "I guess we got most of the wrapping done, but I think we still should meet back here asap. I still need my wingwoman." He winked and smoothed down her hair, which was pleasantly in disarray. "Got a little carried away. Your cheeks are bright pink."

"Duh." She put a hand to her cheek, then fanned the legal pad over her face. "Get that smirk off your face."

Presley opened the door. Dillon and Suzi looked around and tried to wiggle into the room. "Not so fast. We're not done in here."

Halo cleared her throat as she stood behind him as a front, blocking prying eyes from getting a gander at the still-unwrapped Christmas items strewn everywhere. Presley lumbered forward. "Out of here. Scram you two." Halo followed close behind. He scooted the kiddos in one direction, and she closed the door and bolted into the kitchen. Presley gazed over his shoulder, barely able to contain his smile.

HALO SHUFFLED through the boxes and canned goods in the pantry, taking note of the staple items she would need for the recipes she had in mind. She sorted through spices and set ones she needed aside. She opened her phone to find a few recipes and Pinterest projects to keep the kids busy, bubbling with excitement at fun they were going to have.

Halo swiveled around in her chair to find Presley leaning against the door, that freshly showered, strapping man. He was wearing snug jeans that played up his broad shoulders and slim hips.

"I see you still have that smirk on your face. How long have you been standing there?"

"Long enough." He walked to the chair and looked over her shoulder. "Any luck?"

She bit at the lid of the pen. "Yes, I've found several recipes we can make with the food you have here. I can make cookies with the frozen premade dough you have, and bedazzle them up with some of the candy I saw in the other room. The kids could help decorate." Halo looked up at his face, hovering so near her own. "I noticed a ham. Is that for Christmas dinner?"

"Yes, along with veggies and carbs I know the kids will eat. Macaroni and cheese, probably, and I'll think of something to do with the potatoes."

"I can make a dish everyone will love for the potatoes. Do you mind?"

"Go for it. I did buy a gingerbread house we can all do together."

She turned; her eyes wide. "Really? I've always wanted to do one, but haven't."

"Then we must make that a priority. I'm not sure if I've done one since I was a kid, but back then it didn't come in a box. My mom baked everything, and it was a few days' ordeal. I wish you could meet my parents, but the storm blew their travel plans."

"If the storm hadn't happened, I'd be in my little apartment eating Hamburger Helper."

"I love the stuff. You may have found a few boxes in there, and tons of hamburger in the freezer." He patted his stomach. "It's a necessary staple around here."

"Me too and yes, I did. Perfect, that will probably be one meal. But I have other plans first. Some of your perishables will go fast, so I have a few ideas for them."

"I experiment and cook more at the station, but the kids' palette isn't too keen yet. They could live off PB&J, chicken fingers, and macaroni with cheese. I concede and give them what they want."

"Nothing wrong with any of that. We can still do what they like, but it's Christmas, so let's have some fun." *Listen to me! What's this 'we' stuff?*

"Sign me up. I'm getting a little stir crazy being locked up in here. Not used to be sedentary. It's too cold to go out and Champ almost froze his paws when I took him out."

"No worries, Let's see what you have."

He held the small stepladder steady and took her hand as she climbed the steps. "Careful." He put his hands around her hips." I got you."

"I'm counting on it. I'm clumsy." She looked over her shoulder and gave him a wry smile. "True story. You didn't see me slide down your neighbor's hill."

"I'm sorry I missed that, but you did lose your footing on the ice in front of me."

"I crashed and burned. Don't remind me. It was not my proudest moment."

She explored the top shelf, finding baking soda, brown and powdered sugars, cocoa, marshmallows, little cereal boxes, canisters of flour, and an array of other staples. "I think I just hit the motherload. I see great things in our gullets later." Halo handed Presley a few items and he set them aside.

"I'm down for it all. Speaking for my gullet, I will say it thanks you very much."

"You have a ton of paper lunch bags, paper plates, and colorful napkins. Can I use some of these? We could use the kids' markers and crayons for an easy project. Do you have any string?"

"I think I can scrounge up something." He ran a hand over his chin.

"Good. May I take a little seek-and-find for stuff in the kids' rooms?"

"Certainly. I don't think they will mind. I'll distract them so they don't follow you." Presley stuffed his hands deep in his pockets as he listened with intent, intrigued by her enthusiasm.

"I never had much when I was growing up so, I improvised." I can look at anything, pick it apart, and make a stripped-down version, presto." She snapped her fingers. "It comes in handy for entertaining kids in school." Halo rattled on as if she was an open book.

"Have at it, but beware, you may get lost in there." Presley high-fived Halo. "Most of their stuff ends up on the floor. Every time I clean it up it finds its way back under my feet, and I've maimed myself more times than I can count on some doohickey or thingamabob."

Halo's eyes sparkled as she beamed. "You are so funny." She grabbed one of the brown paper lunch bags and shook it open. "*Operation: Seek And Find* is underway."

"I'd wear shoes. You've been warned," he said in jest.

She put a finger to her lips. "Shhh. Be vewy, vewy, quiet, you pesky wabbit."

"Okay, Elmer Fudd," Presley said as he slugged back the last of his drink.

Halo covered her mouth, holding in a chuckle as she darted down the hall to the children's room.

First stop was Suzi's perfectly pink palace with an LED-lit canopy over her bed, fit for a princess. Presley was right. There were a lot of little gadgets and random toys everywhere: a doll's shoe, purse, a baby's bottle, and dress-up clothes. She rifled through a plastic bin to a gold mine of things. Pink and teal feathers from one of Suzi's dress-up boas were scattered everywhere. They would be perfect for the dreamcatcher she wanted the children to make. Halo grabbed a handful here, there, and everywhere. Little eyeball stickers were on Suzi's little plastic table, as were stickers galore. Halo took a couple of wavy art scissors, perfect for Suzi's little hands.

Next was Dillon's room. He was definitely a superhero fan. His room was a little more organized, which fit his big boy demeanor, and his fireman bed warmed her heart. He idolized his father. Halo used her Spidey-sense and sorted through a few sheets of Spiderman and Superman stickers, and others more reminiscent of Mr. Potato Head with ears, mustaches, noses, and hats. Most would be perfect for the brown bag puppets she was planning.

* * *

PRESLEY BRUSHED his little girl's hair meticulously, putting each in little pigtails. Her hair was like corn silk and so fine there wasn't a chance of her hair staying that way. A glint of light hit his wedding ring. He couldn't bring himself to take off. Like ridding the closet of Abby's clothes, it felt permanent. *It is. Nothing more permanent than death.* He cleared his throat in hopes of dismantling the direction his thoughts were heading.

"Kids, you know, I've been thinking." He paused. "Wouldn't it be fun to make something for Halo since it's Christmas and all? Maybe you can draw her a picture or make her a card. I can help you."

Suzi spun around and squealed. "Yes, Daddy, I think it would be fun."

"I can draw real good daddy. I think she would like it, or I can make her an ornament. I have the kit you gave me last year."

"I think that's a great idea. I know she will like whatever you make. But we need to keep it just between us. It must be a surprise."

"Just like the surprise you have for us in your room?"

"Yes, Suzi, but I'll have to figure out how to distract her while you make your surprise. Let me see what I can do. We don't have much time. Tomorrow is Christmas, and we need to make sure she has something to open."

"You can always go back in the room and work on your surprise for us while I help Suzi make something for Miss Halo." Dillon had a huge grin on his face.

"You would do that for her?"

The boy nodded.

"Me too Daddy," Suzi whispered as they all huddled together.

"You could do that on your own without me supervising?"

"I'm a big boy. We could use watercolors and draw. What about a stocking?"

Presley scratched his head. "I'm sure I can think of something for a stocking. Okay, you can start it, let it dry, and maybe I'll help you write what you want to say to her."

Suzi jumped up and down, fisted her little hands in the air, and squealed again. Dillon twirled around with his cape and shot a hand in the air. "Superheroes can do anything! They have superpowers."

Presley put a finger to his lips again and whispered. "Remember, just between us."

The children nodded and ran off to their craft table at the far end of the living room. He needed to sort through the attic for leftover Christmas stuff and come up with a solution while Halo was busy in the kitchen. He peeked in the doorway; she was busy.

"The kids are content for a while, so I'm heading up to the attic.

"I have my hands full and it's amazing."

"No, I got this. You have enough on your plate as it is. You keep up with what you're doing." He crossed his arms over his chest and rocked from heel to toe. "The kids promised me not to interrupt you for a while. Take full advantage of the quiet. Their attention span needs work, so who knows how long it will last? I won't be gone long."

"Not going anywhere. I'll be here when you return."

* * *

HHALO LOVED everything about being in Presley's home, but she had to be dreaming. If it wasn't for the snowstorm and a kind-hearted man taking mercy on her, the two of them would be nowhere near each other's vicinity...well, maybe in Dillon's kindergarten class. She was from the wrong side of the tracks, and that was okay. He had his hands full with his sweet babies. She would make a memory or two and this Christmas was by far a keeper.

Flip the switch, girl. After years of practice, she always had the ability to turn a negative into a positive. *Remember, there's always something to look forward to.*

This would be great practice for when she had her own family and started new traditions. She hummed a Christmas tune and started one of her first meal preps, then gathered the crafts for the first project and put together an interactive dessert the kids could make.

"Fa-la-la-la-la-la...."

Halo turned the music up and sashayed across the room. She flipped around to see a wide-grinned Presley taking in her below-average attempt at a talent show.

"Yup, totally embarrassed." She covered her face with the towel and heard him step closer.

He ran his hands up and down her arms. "Don't be. It's cute."

Just what she wanted to be: cute.

He pulled the towel away from her face. She could feel the fire in her skin as he ran the pad of his thumb along her cheek. "You should never be embarrassed around me. You're safe." She looked at her socked feet, but Presley lifted her chin. "I hate that you've had a life where you don't know that, and you should be reminded every day how very special you are."

"It's okay. I think I'm pretty darn special, but I've made my peace with things I couldn't control. I chose a long time ago to let go of the things that doesn't give me joy, and I'm proud to admit I happily let go. No one ever made me feel special but my parents, whom I barely remember, and my great-aunt. The rest must come internally. I'm still a work in progress."

"Aren't we all. Maybe you have made peace, but I haven't. What little I know about your life, what you endured--no one deserves any part of it. You of all people should have never suffered." He wrapped his arms around Halo and, for the first time since she was a little girl, she felt truly cared for.

Wanting to weep, she held back. Having Presley's massive arms around her soothed her, and she fought the tears. "You are an amazing human, Mr. Devry. Your children are lucky to have you."

He leaned back and inspected her. "You know it's okay to let your guard down. You've seen me at my worst when I had my meltdown when you first arrived, and you called me on it."

"You mean your hissy-fit?"

He nodded. "Right? It was, wasn't it?" He nuzzled closer and massaged her neck. "I have big shoulders. You were there for me, I want to be there for you."

She shivered and wanted to have a class *A* meltdown. She gazed into the depths of his now-familiar eyes, knowing he had his own pain too, but was willing to aid in hers.

"No one can always navigate alone."

"Let's make a pact then. An oath."

"What kind of pact?"

"One where we're honest and, no matter what we say, we always tell each other our thoughts. I'm not sure if I've been truly honest with myself, but with you, I'd like to give it my all."

"Honesty is the best policy. I'll do my best. I've never had someone I could really do that with. It's been hard since it's just been me, myself, and I."

"Probably couldn't hurt either of us. We're stranded together. Plus, I suspect it might do me a whole hell of a lot of good. The more I try to ignore things, the worse they get. To be honest with you, I'm so tired of spinning my wheels. I've been stuck. I want to live; I mean really live. That's one thing I learned after digging deep with the company counselor and after losing Abby. I just didn't know how."

"You owe it to yourself and your children to move forward."

"So do you."

Presley extended his hand. "Do we have a pact, partner?"

"Yes. You've got a deal, pal." She swatted him with the towel and rounded the corner of the counter. He grabbed her by the waist and tickled her before she could escape. She squirmed.

"This will be a great union indeed." He looked over at the children busily working at their craft table. "They're pretty content."

Halo glanced around him. "What are they enthralled by?" She headed in their direction, only to be stopped by Presley.

"Don't be nosy. It's Christmas. While they are busy, I could use help with another wrapping extravaganza. We made progress, but I found more." Presley gave her a lopsided grin and raise his shoulders."

"Let's do it."

He took her hand and snuck off to the spare room with the gifts. "In full exposure, it's a great excuse to get you alone again." He raised his brows up and down.

"I'm not disagreeing with you either. For honesty's sake, I have to say it doesn't feel proper around the kids."

"Do you know how many times they have conspired against me with the neighbors? Tons! I can't even go to the grocery store without the kids embarrassing me by saying someone is pretty all the time, or asking if they want a new husband? And don't get me started on my cousin, Lauren. Parents night at the school is out of control."

Halo covered her mouth and chuckled. "That's hilarious. I guess everyone just wants you to be happy."

He moved closer and wrapped his arms around Halo's waist. "I'm working on my own happy. May I kiss you?"

"No, but I will meet you halfway and we can kiss each other."

"I like the way you think."

* * *

PRESLEY STOKED the flames and placed another log on the fire before heading back into the kitchen. He sipped on his coffee as he watched Halo and the kids make fruit Santas with grapes, strawberries, bananas, and little marshmallows. She held the toothpicks and instructed the kids how to arrange the fruit. Her hair glistened and her eyes were bright. He could see she was having as much fun as they were.

"Let's give your dad a couple to try, and each of you can have one before we start on our next fun project."

"There's more?"

"Of course there is."

"We have a secret too, Miss Halo." Dillon covered his mouth and looked at his dad. "Sorry."

"That's okay, pal."

Halo anchored a hand on her hip and narrowed her eyes at Presley. "A secret? Not fair. That's okay, because the children and I have a secret too and you can't know about either."

"Oh, yeah?" He squinted his eyes and looked to his son and daughter. Both laughed. Halo whispered in one child's ear, then the others. The kids ran into the other room whooping and hollering.

He missed having someone in the house. She was so vivacious, and the walls echoed with laughter. The air felt lighter and joyful for the first time in years. Somehow, he thought if Abby were watching, she'd approve. He dug at his chest. *Yes, she would approve.* The kids were having a blast and so was he.

"Now what?" He looked at his watch. "I think I need to see if

I can get the kiddos nap for a bit. I'm sure they won't sleep, but fingers crossed."

"I could use some quiet time by the fire." Something roared like a freight train, making Halo stand iron straight. She whipped around, her eyes wide. "What just slammed against your house?" Her teeth chattered, and she covered her ears at the howling. "Is that the wind?"

"I'm afraid so. It's getting colder." He inched his way to the window, pulling the old blue checkered curtain aside. His failed attempt to wipe the condensation away from the window backfired; it had crystalized into ice and his hand almost stuck to it. He wiped his hand on his denim. "This storm is a doozy. We haven't seen nothing like this in years."

"Worse?" she stammered. "It's frigid just standing nearby. I didn't know it would be like this. They make it look so serene on television." She wrapped her arms tighter around herself.

Presley knew he shouldn't sugarcoat the severity. She needed to be informed that no one messed around with these storms. The thought of her in peril made him nauseous, and the pulse in his neck revved up a notch. He ran his hand along his stomach.

"It's inviting as long as you are prepared and in a warm house, but it's very dangerous out in the elements, so dangerous you could get hypothermia," he said, as if he was giving a speech to new recruits. "It's rough, being on shift out there when the bad weather rolls in. We've had to get the snowcat and dig out stranded motorists. At least with this storm, we got the heads up that it was blasting our way. It hit Colorado and the Rocky Mountains first and closed Denver for several days. Usually melts faster there than it does here. Made its way through Nebraska." He shook his head and squinted. "Sorry. Always the first responder, I guess."

"Very informative." She winced and hugged her midsection. "I hope no one is stuck out there." She bit at her thumbnail.

"Me too, but if they were, the guys at the station probably have them nestled at home already."

"I worry about your neighbors."

He blew out his cheeks. "Those two? Not a chance. They are resilient. Trudged over here to drop off the furballs, remember?" He crinkled his eyes and scratched his head. "Come to think of it, I'm uncertain how they got themselves and two kittens in a big box to my front door, then disappeared before we saw them. And in a snowstorm."

"That's right. How could I forget?" Halo wrapped a sweater around her shoulders and tucked her feet under her on the couch. "I can't imagine them making it out of their house and over here without injury. I bruised my pride getting here, and it was a long way down that hill."

He cleared his throat and his eyes crinkled at the corners. "Your pride, huh? I'll go look in on the kiddos."

* * *

PRESLEY CAME BACK. "They're sound asleep." He grabbed the remote control and turned the local news on. The lights flickered. "Yikes, some areas are losing power," he called over his shoulder. "I'll get the emergency candles and flashlights ready, just in case we have a power outage. We're set for firewood, so we will be warm and have a little ambient light."

Halo laughed nervously. "I'm used to it happening in the South with storms. I guess I never thought it would be as dangerous with the snow." Her hand cupped over her mouth and she fought for words. *I'm going to die in a bomb cyclone.* She darted her gaze one way, then another. Her heart thumped wildly and battered in her chest.

Presley stopped mid-step and locked gazes her. "Halo. It's okay." The soft sound of his voice reached her ears. "Look at me." He pointed to his eyes. "Nothing will happen, I promise."

He ran his hands along her arms. "Come sit." He guided her to the chair.

She shook her head to snap out of it, but her legs didn't comply. *You got this, girl.* "With all the ruckus out there, I can't figure out what's louder, the howling outside or my teeth chattering." *Summon your inner warrior.* She shot out of the chair.

"First, I'll recheck the pipes, make sure they're wrapped tight so they don't bust. It's supposed to drop below zero overnight."

"You don't have to go outside, do you?" She paced back and forth, wringing her hands.

"I'm afraid so. While I'm at it, I better let Champ out to do his business."

"Be careful." She winced. "Better skedaddle, I'll boil water for hot cocoa and check on the casserole in the oven. It should be close to done, but we should keep it warm. I'm sure when the kids wake up, they will be famished. Maybe I'll throw in a few cookies too. Fingers crossed the electricity stays on." She paced back and forth, not sure what direction to head.

"Beware. Those kids can sniff out cookies a mile away," Presley laughed. "I'll get you a couple of thermoses. Best we're prepared."

* * *

HALO CLEARED the dishes off the table as Presley pulled the last sheet of cookies from the oven. The lights flickered again, this time only to stay off. Complete darkness surrounded them and Suzi wailed. Presley lit the nearby candle. He could see Halo's silhouette flattened against the wall, shivering. He scooped up his daughter. "Halo, give me your hand. Come on. I've got you." He weaved her fingers through his and drew her close. "Dillon, how are you, buddy?"

"I'm not afraid."

"Good, pal. I didn't think so, but it's okay if you were. Can you bring me the flashlight right beside the table? I need your help. We must light as many candles as we can, so Suzi isn't afraid." Presley said in a calm voice.

"We can't play with fire. You said so," Dillon replied.

"You're right. How about this? I'll light the candles and you can set them up with Miss Halo if you are careful," he spoke in his composed tone. The boy handed him the flashlight and he turned it on, pointing it around the room. "Hey, I have an idea. Who wants to camp out in front of the fire?"

Dillon screeched. "With smores and a blanket tent?"

Presley grimaced at the thought. "What do I always say about open flames?"

"Safety first and stay away" Dillon replied. He tipped his head and winked at his son. "You got that right. Can you help me out, fella? We need to gather blankets and pillows for everyone."

The boy nodded with enthusiasm.

"It might get cold, so we all need to stay together in the living room and close off all of our bedrooms." Presley grabbed an armload of blankets and pillows to put in front of the fireplace. After lighting the candles, Halo found her way to the couch with Suzi comforting the girl. It might have been the other way around; no one was certain. Both looked content.

"Daddy, do we get to sleep here tonight?"

"Maybe so, pal. If the electricity stays off, we need to monitor the fire. It will be warmer there."

"I'm scared." Suzi scooted onto Halo's lap.

She patted the little girl. "Me too, but nothing will happen to us if we are together. Your father will protect all of us. Remember, that's what he does."

Presley gave a snort. "What if I'm scared? Who's gonna save me?" He moved the coffee table aside and laid out several heavy-duty blankets in front of the couch, then a sheet and more blankets, lining the pillows along the front of the couch. "Here's an extra for you, Halo."

"Why can't I sleep on the floor with everyone else? So not fair."

"Yay, Daddy! We're camping with Miss Halo," Dillon shouted.

* * *

THE NEXT MORNING, Halo squirmed but couldn't move. She played back the festivities from the night before. A night where laughter had been abundant, with songs, stories, games galore, cocoa and dessert by fire. Slowly opening her eyes, Halo could only see that Suzi's locks were a rotisserie of crazy in her face. The little girl was draped over her. She tried to wiggle her arm free, but it was asleep under the weight of Champ and the little boy using him as a pillow. She heard a motorboat of purring in her ear where one kitten nuzzled up close and personal.

The other was curled up in a ball on Presley's chest. Her heart battered wildly at how close he was. She scanned up his chest. Holy—heavenly—hotness. His arms were folded over his thick chest, his muscles flexed, a sprinkle of dark blond hair peeking out of his form fitting shirt. His Adam's apple bobbed with each breath. The cords of his neck spoke power and the prickly facial hair over chiseled jaw was awe-inspiring. His full pink lips gave her pause.

She tried to calm her breathing, but it was a loss after looking at Mr. Sassy Pants. He looked so peaceful; she could gaze at him forever. He shifted, turning onto his side and leaning on one elbow. Halo shut her eyes and pretended to be asleep. Presley inched closer. She could feel the warmth of his breath at her ear. "I know you're awake," he said in a low, smoky whisper, unraveling her last speck of composure.

She jolted. "Geez! I didn't know you were awake," she whispered, attempting to pull the cover over her head with her free arm.

"You appeared to be enjoying yourself. I didn't want to intrude whatever fantasy you're conjuring up, or at least I hoped."

Halo could feel the heat creep along her cheeks. *Busted.*

His jaw ticked. "Besides, I'm a light sleeper. When the kids are zonked out, they can sleep through anything." He yawned. "I deliberately kept them up late. As much as I enjoy all of us laying here, my back is killing me." He smiled and kissed her cheek. "I'd love nothing more than hang here, but it's Christmas and we have celebrating to do. Santa presents under the tree and pronto. I'm not sure how much time we have. I may need a hand."

"I only have one useable one momentarily. I'm stuck in a dog pile and my arm is asleep."

Presley wiggled out from under the blankets and set the kitten aside. He got on his knees, hoisting his son off Champ and laying him near the big beast. Dillon didn't stir. "Psst. Champ, come here." Presley snapped his fingers and crawled around to the other side of Halo as the dog followed, wagging his tail. Presley picked up his daughter, carefully laying her beside her brother. He stretched his hand out and helped guide Halo up.

"Merry Christmas."

She noticed the lights of the Christmas tree twinkling. "Hey, the power is back. It is a Merry Christmas indeed."

"Good. I need a cup of joe."

Warmth spread through her with all the excitement of Christmas. It was perfect already. They tiptoed through the kitchen to the seasonal porch and the stockpile of goodies in Presley's room. Each of their arms was loaded to the hilt. She giggled carefully, trying not to drop anything. They carefully inched their way to the tree, setting the gifts underneath it.

"I have the kiddos' stockings and I may need some muscle for Suzi's doll house. Dillon has a bike in the garage."

"I'm a pro at moving. I have muscles and here's the proof." She lifted her arms and flexed.

Presley squeezed her triceps. "Look at those guns."

She pawed at him and chuckled. "Oh stop."

No sooner was everything situated under and around the tree, Presley snuck something he had hidden behind his back, hanging it on the back of the tree. He rustled the children awake and they sprang into action. They were wide-eyed at their Santa gifts, bringing Dillon to tears with his new bike.

"A bike with no training wheels?"

"Don't you think you need a big bike because you are a big boy?"

Dillon leaped into his dad's arms. Halo bit at her bottom lip and slid her hands along her sweatpants. Suzi inspected every room of her doll house with wonderment. Halo felt such joy as they flung wrapping paper in the air and rummaged through their gifts.

"Miss Halo," Dillon shouted, "there's a gift for you." He skipped to where she was sitting. Halo looked at a small gift. "It's from me. I wrapped it, too."

Halo stared at the interesting technique. The boy had definitely wrapped the gift, but it was the most precious thing she had ever seen. She didn't care what the contents were. Sweet Dillon—all his freckles, cocoa still around his mouth, his hair having a Beetlejuice moment—nothing compared to his pride-filled expression at being a gift bearer.

Tears threatened as her vision as she held it tight, bringing it to her chest. "You didn't need to give me anything." She stuttered to get the words out. "I know I will love it."

"Open it." The boy jumped up and down with excitement.

She ripped the wrapping paper away to find a small wood

ornament in red and blue with a little picture of Dillon glued to it.

"I signed the back," he said, pointing to the other side.

She turned it over. "I love it so much. I will cherish it always."

He handed her the card he had made too, covered with tons of stickers on the front and the back.

Miss Halo,

Thank you for spending Christmas with us and making Daddy smile. He's handsome when he's happy.

P.S. Daddy helped me with the big words, but he didn't want to write handsome.

Love Dillon.

She traced over his words. "Love it." Halo looked at the little boy, who was beaming with pride at his handy work.

Suzi scampered forward and handed Halo a gift. "I made you a gift, too."

She opened the bag and untied the ribbon. Her ornament was bedazzled with everything glittery and sparkly, just like the little girl who made it. Hers was pink and purple with mounds of glitter glue, and it might have been a little wet still.

"It's so pretty!" Halo giggled. "You did this all by yourself?"

The little girl nodded and gave her a toothless grin. "I made you a card too, but Daddy had to help me with all the words."

Halo gazed over at Presley as he smirked. "And I had to write everything she said, too."

She inspected the front of the card, which had several stick figures on the front. When she opened the card, she noticed two more stick figure girls. The words got her choked up, knowing Presley and Suzi worked together. "Appears she isn't at a loss for words."

"I had to stop her before it became *War and Peace*." Presley shot out of his chair and paced, avoiding eye contact.

Miss Halo,

I'm glad we're friends. Thank you for letting me help you in the kitchen with the dishes. You make me happy. I want to color, make snow angels, dress up, have tea parties. I know I have been a good girl, and I asked Santa for a special gift. I don't want to be the only girl anymore, then it can be boys against the girls. Will you be my mommy?

Love, Suzi.

Halo coughed and blinked away the tears forming in her eyes. She covered her face, and a sob came out.

Dillon ran to get a tissue and handed it to her.

"Suzi, you asked Santa for a mommy?"

The girl nodded. "Since Mommy is in heaven, I want you to be our new mommy." She snuggled closer. "I ask almost every year since Mommy left us, but this year I prayed too that someone would come along. Daddy doesn't like other ladies, but he likes you. He said so." The girl leaped on Halo's lap and hugged her tight.

"Thank you so much. I appreciate your gift and card." Halo cleared her throat. "Shall we give your dad his gifts?" She cast a glance in Presley's direction.

He slugged back his last bit of coffee. "Presents? For moi?"

Halo nodded and sprung up to meet him. He was looking around at everything but her.

"Presley?" He jumped and brought her to focus as she smiled. "It must have been awkward for you to write what Suzi wanted. I'm sorry."

"Don't be. The card was my idea in the first place. Serves me right. A little embarrassment is healthy. I hope it didn't make you uncomfortable."

"Not in the least." Halo guessed the opposite was true for him.

"My daughter can be very convincing, and she has me

wrapped around her little finger." He chuckled. "Out of the mouth of babes."

She put a finger in the air. "I'll go get your presents."

Halo returned with the gifts she'd hidden behind the tree and waved them in the air. "Here you go. Do you want your dad to open these?" She glanced at Presley again. "You may want to sit for this. With the first gift you open, the kids have a little performance to share."

"Yippee." Suzi shouted at the top of her lungs. Dillon and Suzi grabbed their gifts. "Daddy, this one first." She squealed a high-pitched ear splitter.

Halo covered her ears and mouthed the word *wow.*

He shoved his fingers in his ears. "Shhh…" He winced. "I wish I could say one gets used to it, but that would be a lie. Inside voices, kiddos."

Presley opened the little box and spotted several brown paper bags made in an array of characters for a puppet show. He lifted one that had bright flames, eyeballs, a nose, and an array of stickers on it. "Daddy, this one is you," Dillon said in a deep voice, "and the others are me, Suzi, Champ, Willy and Wonka."

"You named the cats?"

"Guess why we named them that?"

"I have a pretty good guess. Does it have anything to do with chocolate?"

"Yay!"

Presley clapped his hands together after the kids performed their puppet show, which was mostly meowing and barking. Halo handed him the other gift. He looked at the tag.

To Daddy from your kids, with help from your houseguest.

She bounced her legs up and down nervously.

He opened it and lifted it up. "I've seen these before."

"It started off as a dreamcatcher, then we changed direction. The children had other ideas. It can be whatever you want it to be. Remember the project we were going to do? The kids wanted to make one for you." She pointed to a few things she had gathered around the house. "It's 100 percent recycled, full of good wishes and energy, and made with love for your wildest dreams to come true."

Hours came and went while Halo watched as Presley and the children played together. No matter how hard she wished, she didn't belong here, and she was getting too close. She was still the outsider. There was a black moment looming, the rug pull where everything was ripped away and like always it was coming. In the past someone else made the decision. Not today, she was in control, and she made her own. Halo had to make an exit as soon as the weather allowed. She couldn't help from feeling. Why did this hurt so much?

Presley and his family were so easy to love. *Love?* Why would she know anything about love? But that's exactly what she felt. She didn't belong here. They were polar opposites. It was the truth and it still stung. She wrung her hands together and bounced her knee up and down.

I never belong—anywhere.

Why would Presley ever want her. She had to get out while she could walk out on her own accord. *I must.*

* * *

TWO DAYS AFTER CHRISTMAS, the snow stopped and began to melt. The temperature rose and the sun was shining. The call came from the local garage and Presley's gut twisted. He'd had more days than he imagined with Halo, but it was time for her to leave and he dreaded it.

"Bernie's Garage called. They can tow your car there and see what it needs. If you like, I can give you a ride." His tongue stuck to the roof of his mouth and his chest felt heavy.

"Don't be silly. I'll have them drop me off on the way. You have done so much for me already."

"I really don't mind." Presley paced back and forth. He had to think fast. He was close to a panic. He had gotten so used to having her around, and he didn't want to lose their connection.

"I better gather the clothes you gave me. Thank you again."

"Of course. I'm glad you'll get good use of them. Whatever you don't need, I can donate. If you forget anything, you could always come back." He was nearing a full- blown ramble session.

"I'd love nothing more."

"Halo, can I ask you something?"

"Sure." She scrunched her nose and smiled.

"What are your plans for New Year's Eve?"

She hesitated. "I'll have to check my imaginary schedule." A second passed and she blurted out. "No calendar, so no plans."

"You do now. I'd like to take you out on a date. We haven't had our first one."

"What do you mean, Mr. Devry? We've had the best one ever, and it lasted a week. You're going to have a tough time topping it."

He winked. "Probably so, but I'm up for the task, if you'll give it a whirl."

She rolled her eyes. "That's a no-brainer. You saved my life."

* * *

HALO PACKED the last of her things and decided something needed to be said. More for her than the receiver, but important just the same.

Writing was a much easier way to express her deepest thoughts and feelings. Climbing the stairs slowly, she felt cloaked in so many raw emotions.

You would think leaving another house would be easier by now after all the practice, but this place is special. They are special.

She tiptoed by the Christmas tree and felt so inadequate,

looking at one of the decorations that said *Mommy* on it. *I don't belong here. This is Abby's house; her memory is everywhere.* Halo placed the note in the delicate ornament and replaced it in the tree, saying a silent prayer for all the gifts she received over the past week. Most of them had nothing to do with bows and paper.

Halo hugged the children, making her way outside. *I loved being here.* She stood at the end of the drive as she and Presley watched her car being secured to the back of the tow truck.

She thought of everything that had transpired between them. The light of the sun was blinding, so she squinted and took one step closer to Presley.

"Thank you for opening your home and giving me the best Christmas I've ever had. My first snow angel experience was spectacular and building a snowman was superb." She gave a forced laugh, clearing the sorrow she was attempting to swallow. Humor was her only hope for getting through this moment. She took a huge inhale and let it out. "You are one of the kindest men I have ever met. You could have judged me for the life I had, but you opened your home with nothing but care and respect. I will always be grateful for your hospitality." Halo caught a glimpse of the front window of the house. She witnessed both children waving. She blew kisses and waved them goodbye, but they started bawling. She clutched her chest. "Oh no. Suzi and Dillon are crying," she said with a long face.

Presley swung around. "Can the kids come out for another hug?"

"Of course. I could use one."

He jogged up the drive and into the house.

* * *

"Kids, get your coats on and say another goodbye to Halo before she leaves." Presley eyed something in the tree as he pulled their coats on. "You go on out. I'll be right there. Miss Halo said she will wait."

He reached for the ornament with a scrolled paper hanging out of the top and pulled it from the branches. Unfolding the note, his heart stilled when he noticed it was addressed to Abby.

Dearest Abby,

I don't know why I was compelled to write this. You don't know me, but I had the distinct honor of being in your home with your husband and beautiful children. I wish I could have met you because the love I've witnessed shows me you were very special.

I've heard so much about you and, by the look in your family's eyes, I know you were loved.

Maybe you are watching over them. I hope so. It keeps me going. I believe my parents and great auntie look over me. I can't express what being here has meant, but I was blessed beyond measure to experience what true love is. Your family made my Christmas wish come true.

Presley adored you. I hope I find that kind of love, and I pray one day he will find his happily ever after. I'll be watching closely to make sure your kids have someone worthy of all their love. They have worked their way into my heart. It breaks me that your beautiful babies lost you so young. I know how much it hurts.

Thank you seems so little, but I felt you everywhere. Your children are an extension of you and your legacy. I truly enjoyed every moment with them. It was a pleasure. Merry heavenly Christmas, Abby.

Love and admiration,

Halo Wrightway

PRESLEY SET THE NOTE ASIDE, laid something on it, and snatched what he had stashed behind the tree. He hurried outside. *Halo deserves the truth. I promised her.* The kids were already standing alongside Halo as she spun them around. She gazed upon him as he approached, and he never felt surer.

Halo hugged the children close. "I will cherish the gifts all of you made for me. They will go on my refrigerator so I can see them every day." She brushed at her nose with her mitten.

The tow truck driver sounded his horn and waved her on. She backed away slowly. "I'm awful with goodbyes, so for now, see ya later." She bent down and squeezed Dillon's cheeks. "I will see you in school." She hugged Suzi one last time and wrapped her arms around Presley. He stayed silent and held her tight. She pulled away.

No. I need you.

One step became two, and then another, and then she made it to the front of the tow truck. Presley shouted her name at the top of his lungs.

She whipped around and he jogged to her. He never felt surer of anything in his life. *I'm ready.*

"Please don't go, Halo. I forgot something." He picked her up and swung her around, nestling his face to her ear, righting her on the ground. He handed her the red and white stocking. "It's for you."

"For me? I don't understand."

He held it over his heart. "I don't want you to leave." He swallowed hard and held her hands, never wanting to let go. "I don't think I can bear it. I already miss you," he said as he stammered, and his voice broke.

* * *

Halo glanced at his hands as he gripped the stocking, noticing something missing. Presley's wedding ring. Her gaze shot back to him, and her mouth hung open.

His soulful eyes penetrated her. His look was one of vulnerability, desperation, and elation.

"I'm ready. It's you I want." His bottom lip quivered. "I can't go back to my life before I met you. Please, if you will have me."

He stalled mid-sentence and turned back to his children. "I mean us. We will show you every day how much you are loved."

Presley was her Christmas miracle, and he wanted her. *Is this my happily-ever-after? Me. Someone wants me.* She bobbed her head in agreement as a smile lifted the corners of her mouth. "Oh, I'm not going anywhere. Your attempts will be futile. Just try to get rid of me." She laughed and kissed him madly.

He squeezed her tight, and she knew this kiss meant so much more.

Mine.

"Never gonna happen. You're ours, Halo Wrightway. I love you."

Merry Christmas!
May the spirit of the holidays always be in your heart.

To their beginning...

ABOUT THE AUTHOR

Jodi James was born in California, raised in the heartland of Iowa, and lives in sunny Florida with her husband and fur kids Romeo and Guinness. Blessed with a successful career in the hair and beauty industry spanning over three decades.
She's fulfilling a lifelong passion for writing. Her journey has transcended and evolved from reading to being inspired by the authors that wrote the words. She writes about perseverance, positivity, and passion.
Her first published short story, The Rest Is Still Unwritten, was included in an anthology with The Heart of Denver Romance Writers. In The Heat Of It All was her first Contemporary Romantic Suspense novel and the first in the Brothers of Solemn Creed series, followed by To The Core, One Night, and At The The End Of The Day. Legacy is an added prequel to her series.
She believes in the happily-ever-after. Writing makes her heart sing.

JOIN JODI ONLINE

AUTHORJODIJAMES.COM

Keep up with Jodi and join her newsletter. https://
authorjodijames.com/newsletters/

Linktree
https://linktr.ee/jodijames

Facebook
Instagram
BookBub
Twitter

AFTERWORD

I hope you enjoyed *Merry Frickin' Christmas* by Jodi James. Be sure to leave a review.

Do you want to join my street team?
Show me some love and follow me on Facebook in my private group. Jodi's Hot Zone

This group is a place of positivity and empowerment for strong women and the book boyfriends who light up their lives.

Do you want to hang out with the author and her tribe, win book prizes, see cover reveals first, have fun, and support Jodi's books on social media? Join Jodi's reader group on Facebook: JodiJamesHotZone

ACKNOWLEDGMENTS

I'm a family first kind of girl, and I'd like to thank my peeps for their unwavering support and love. Your strength and cheerleading pushed me when fear and doubt derailed the process.

Mom, I'm still making my heart sing. Thank you for being my biggest fan. You are my most valued asset and I am blessed beyond measure.

To my husband Tim, you are my best friend, advocate, and supporter. You are the heart of all my stories and everything good. You taught me the true meaning of love and respect. I hope you are proud of me.

To my fur baby's Romeo and Guinness, you are such patient, happy boys. Thank you for being my companions as I write my books. You have taught me to see the beauty that surrounds us.

To the Dream Team, you are my tribe and my soul sisters. I've never met such loving, giving women, and it is truly an honor to know you. I am stronger knowing you have my back. I'm privileged to be in your circle. Much love and admiration.

Lisa O'Neil, thank you for all your posts in my social media readers' group Jodi's Hot Zone. You make waking up a pleasure, you bring happy into our world. I am beyond blessed to know such a beautiful soul.

To all the Hotties in the Zone, thank you for supporting me. You are the genuine heroes. Your kindness makes this world a better place.

To the members of Romance Writers of the Rockies and Florida West Coast Writers, thank you for teaching me the value of community.

To my right-hand powerhouse Virtual Assistant extraordinaire, Kelly Johnson at Cornerstone Virtual Assisting. I won the lottery with you. Thank you for holding my hand through many firsts. I can't imagine my life without you.

Thank you to my cover designer Megan Parker Squires at Em Cat Designs for Merry Frickin' Christmas, Crazy Thing Called Love, and five 'Brothers of Solemn Creed' covers. Thank you for making my vision come to life.

Thank you to my editor Karie Crawford at Cookie Lynn Publishing, you have made such a difference in my writing journey. Thank you for bringing my stories to new heights.

ALSO BY JODI JAMES

www.AuthorJodiJames.com

Legacy (Prequel to the Brothers of Solemn Creed)

Book 1 In The Heat Of It All

Book 2 To The Core

Book 3 One Night

Book 4 At The End Of The Day

Legacy

books2read.com/LegacyPrequel

In The Heat of it all

https://books2read.com/InTheHeatOfItAll

To The Core

https://books2read.com/ToTheCore

One Night

https://books2read.com/OneNightBook3

At The End Of The Day

https://books2read.com/AtTheEndOfTheDay

If you like stories like Merry Frickin' Christmas, stay tuned for the continuation of 'Crazy Thing Called Love' in 2023, currently in the Unleashed Charity Anthology.

To my Readers,

Thank you so much for your support and interest in my books. The Brothers in Solemn Creed has been a labor of love. I so loved writing Merry Frickin' Christmas and Crazy Thing Called Love.Thank you for giving me this opportunity to share my stories. I can't thank you enough.